Lindsey had been lucky so far.

She hadn't seen a sign of Royce in the swamp. After checking to make sure the can of Mace was still tucked into her back pocket, she started retracing her steps, searching for the bright yellow ribbons she'd used to mark her way.

She found the first one. Not far away, she found the second. There the trail ended. Lindsey turned in a circle, looking for a flash of color. They *had* to be here. She'd tied them securely and at regular intervals. She'd been very careful, knowing they would guide her back to safety. They couldn't have disappeared into thin air.

"Looking for these?"

She jumped, startled by Royce's voice. As always, he seemed to materialize out of nowhere, appearing before her like a ghostly wraith. He held out his hand, which was clenched into a fist, the yellow ribbons spilling out like snakes escaping a basket.

Dear Reader,

This month we welcome you to a new venture from Silhouette Books—Shadows, a line designed to send shivers up your spine and chill you even while it thrills you. These are romances, but romances with a difference. That difference is in the fear you'll feel as you journey with the heroine to the dark side of love ... then emerge triumphantly into the light. Who *is* the Shadows hero? Is he on the side of the angels? Sometimes. But sometimes neither you nor the heroine can be sure and you wonder, *Does he want to kiss me—or kill me?*

And what a lineup of authors we have for you. This month we're bringing you *four* tantalizing, terrifying titles by authors you won't be able to resist. Heather Graham Pozzessere is known to romance readers everywhere, but in *The Last Cavalier* she demonstrates an ability to spook you that will ... well ... haunt you long after you've turned the last page. In *Who Is Deborah?,* Elise Title gives her heroine amnesia, leading her to wonder if the man who claims they are married is telling the truth. Because if he's not, what on earth happened to his real wife? Lee Karr's *Stranger in the Mist* mingles past, present and future into a heady brew that will leave you guessing until the very end. And in *Swamp Secrets,* Carla Cassidy creates one of the darkest—and sexiest!— heroes I've seen in a long, long time.

And that's only the beginning! Because from now on we'll be bringing you two Shadows novels every month, novels where fear mingles with passion to create a reading experience you'll find nowhere else. And the authors who will be penning these books are some of the best anywhere. In months to come you'll find books by Jane Toombs, Helen R. Myers, Rachel Lee, Anne Stuart, Patricia Simpson, Regan Forest and Lori Herter, to name only a few. So now, step into the shadows and open yourself up to romance as you've never felt it before—on the dark side of love.

Yours,

Leslie J. Wainger
Senior Editor and Editorial Coordinator

CARLA CASSIDY

Swamp Secrets

Published by Silhouette Books New York

America's Publisher of Contemporary Romance

SILHOUETTE BOOKS
300 East 42nd St., New York, N.Y. 10017

SWAMP SECRETS
Silhouette Shadows #4

Copyright © 1993 by Carla Bracale

ISBN: 0-373-27004-6

First Silhouette Books printing March 1993

Printed in the U.S.A.

Books by Carla Cassidy

Silhouette Shadows

Swamp Secrets #4

Silhouette Romance

Patchwork Family #818
Whatever Alex Wants... #856
Fire and Spice #884
Homespun Hearts #905
Golden Girl #924

Silhouette Desire

A Fleeting Moment #784

CARLA CASSIDY

is the author of many young adult novels, as well as contemporary romances. She's been a cheerleader for the Kansas City Chiefs football team and has traveled the East Coast as a singer and dancer in a band, but the greatest pleasure she's had is in creating romance and happiness for readers.

For my critique group: for all the pain you've caused me!

CHAPTER ONE

The house sat perilously close to the edge of the swamp, as if fighting a losing battle against the gloom that radiated from the dark, thick woods.

Lindsey Witherspoon slowly drove into the driveway and parked. She pulled a sheet of paper out of her purse and rechecked the address, although there was no doubt in her mind that this was Cindy's house. Only Cindy Mae Clairbourne, with her flair for the dramatic, would choose to live in a house perched at the edge of a swamp.

Lindsey turned off the engine and sat for a moment, looking at the house where she would be staying for the next six weeks. The house itself was huge, a Southern-style mansion with a sweeping veranda that in any other setting would look dignified and stately. However, in this particular place, shadowed by huge pine trees and viewed in the eerie glow of twilight, the house seemed foreboding.

With a small laugh of self-derision, she got out of the car and stretched. Obviously she was more tired from the drive than she'd thought.

She found the key just where Cindy had written it would be, beneath a planter on the front porch. She unlocked the door and pushed it open, greeted by the hot, stale air of a house closed up for several days.

As she walked in, she fought against a sense of unease. Inside, the house was decorated beautifully, but with the heavy wooden shutters tightly closed at each window, no sunlight peeked in to lighten the gloom. She walked from room to room, unlocking and shoving open the wooden shutters, allowing in the jasmine-scented breeze and the sunshine.

She found evidence in the decor that Cindy Mae had changed little from when the two women had been roommates in college. She still apparently had a penchant for blue and peach, as most of the rooms sported the pleasing colors.

Lindsey caught her breath as she walked into one of the bedrooms, deciding this would be the one she would sleep in for the duration of her stay. Sunshine seeped in around the edges of the shutters, casting dancing shadows on the furniture. Lindsey threw open the shutter, raising her face to the sunlight that chased away the shadows and the last of her unease.

The room was gorgeous, boasting a canopy bed covered in a pastel-blue spread, and an antique dresser with a large, slightly warped mirror. But it was the French doors that led out to a small balcony that overlooked the back grounds that made Lindsey's decision to claim this room as her own.

She'd always wanted a room with a balcony.

She stepped outside and breathed deeply, smelling the heavy, perfumed scent of strange vegetation, the moist dankness of slow-moving water. It wasn't an unpleasant scent, just different than anything she'd ever smelled before.

The swimming pool was directly below, the water catching the last rays of the sun. Beyond the pool, landscaped grass intermingled with brilliant-colored flowers. Then the swamp, dark and mysterious, with dead cypress trees rising like giant toothpicks and Spanish moss hanging like shrouds. The swamp was already black with the coming of night, its shadows reaching out to claim all that lay nearby. It was almost as if the darkness didn't come from the fading of day, but generated from the swamp itself.

Lindsey shivered and wrapped her arms around herself, finding beauty in the scene despite the chill that danced up her spine. She wished she had her camera handy, but it was still packed in the trunk of her car along with her luggage. She'd love to get a shot of the swamp. *There will be time enough for that later,* she thought, once again taking a deep breath.

Cindy's invitation to house-sit while she and her husband, Remy, were in Europe, had been a godsend. Lindsey needed time to think, evaluate where she was going with her life, what she wanted for herself.

Besides, the swamp would be a perfect place to indulge her passion for photography. She'd always been intrigued by the image of a swamp, although this was as close as she'd ever been to one.

Realizing it would soon be completely dark, she turned and left the balcony. She wanted to get her luggage in before it got too late.

A few minutes later, bags safely deposited in the bedroom, she made herself a drink at the bar in the living room, then turned on the light that illuminated the pool area.

Outside, she sank into one of the chaise longues and leaned her head back with a sigh. This six weeks would be good for her. She needed time away from her life back in Washington, D.C., time to lick her wounds and regain her equilibrium. This Louisiana bayou was as good a place as any to have a personal crisis.

She sighed again and moved the handle to recline the lounger. She closed her eyes, intrigued by the night sounds emanating from the nearby swamp. There was no sound of civilization, no automobile noises to shatter the night creatures' whispers.

She must have fallen asleep because she awoke suddenly, for a moment disoriented as to where she was. Night had embraced the area while she slept. No lingering glow of dusk pierced the grounds beyond where the pool light illuminated.

Yet what instantly disturbed her was the silence. The night sounds that had lulled her to sleep were gone, replaced by a quiet so profound it was unnatural. Even the light breeze that had caressed her face before had stopped. It was as if everything held its breath in anxious anticipation.

The hairs on Lindsey's arms rose as if in response to some electrical field, but she knew it was a reaction to the feeling of being watched. She pulled herself up to a sitting position, trying to pierce the veil of darkness that lay beyond the cocoon of light where she sat.

"Hello?" Her voice sounded small, tinny in the total silence. She squinted, sensing something . . . someone nearby. "Is somebody there?" She projected more force into her tone and was pleased by the effect, then jumped as a twig snapped and footsteps whispered against the grass.

Fear speared through her as she realized how vulnerable she was, how isolated. The nearest neighbor's house was several miles down the road, and the small town of Baton Bay was a twenty-minute drive north. She was completely and totally alone. Nobody would hear her scream.

She reached down and grabbed the drink glass she'd brought outside with her. She needed something in her hands, something that could be used as a weapon.

She stood up, adrenaline pumping through her. "Who's there?" Impatience battled her fear as she shielded her eyes, trying to see beyond the glare of the pool lights. "Cindy, is that you?" she called illogically.

"I'm looking for Remy."

The deep voice reached out of the darkness from behind her, surprisingly close to where she stood, making her jump and whirl around in alarm.

He cloaked himself in the darkness, wearing the shadows like a shield of invisibility. The only thing she could discern about him was his height . . . tall . . . and his shoulders were ominously broad.

"Who...I..." She was appalled to hear her voice come out as a breathless squeak.

"I'm sorry, I didn't mean to frighten you," he said, but his tone held no note of apology.

"I... You merely startled me," Lindsey exclaimed, tightening her grip on the drink glass, although she had a feeling the fragile glass would be quite ineffective against this man who'd appeared out of nowhere.

"Would you mind stepping into the light? It's rather disconcerting to be talking to a disembodied voice in the dark," she said.

"Certainly." He stepped forward and Lindsey instantly wished he'd remained in the shadows.

The light played on his long hair, trying unsuccessfully to pull a highlight from the unrelenting blackness. His face was one that compelled, all harsh angles and planes unrelieved by any hint of softness. As he took a step closer to her she noticed that his eyes were the color of swamp moss, a deep mysterious green. He was hauntingly handsome, carrying himself with a rigid control that somehow suggested an imminent eruption.

Lindsey unconsciously took a step backward, finding his illuminated face strangely disturbing.

"Remy? Is he here?"

Options battled in Lindsey's head. If she said Remy was home, then what excuse could she give for not going inside and getting him? On the other hand, she wasn't sure she liked the idea of this man knowing she would be alone in the house for the next six weeks. She quickly settled somewhere in between. "Cindy and Remy aren't here right now. Perhaps I can tell them you stopped by, Mr. . . . ?"

"Blanchard. Royce Blanchard." His piercing eyes studied her, again causing a shiver of apprehension to work its way up her back. There was something about him that frightened her, an edge of madness in his gaze that unsettled her. Perhaps if he smiled, she thought. Surely that would relieve some of the harshness, minimize the predatory look in his strange eyes.

"What did you do, Mr. Blanchard? Walk through the swamp to get here?" Lindsey forced a smile to her lips, hoping to pull an answering one from him. She would just feel better if he smiled.

"I didn't come through the swamp. I came from it," he answered, no humor apparent. "I live there."

"In the swamp? Really?" For a moment Lindsey's fear abated as a sudden thought struck her. "Then you must know the swamp very well."

"As much as one can. She guards her secrets well."

Lindsey's gaze went out to the darkness, out where the swamp lay with all its mysteries. He made it sound like a living, breathing entity. In fact, if she listened very hard she had the feeling she would be able to hear it breathe, feel its heartbeat.

She looked back at him hesitantly, wondering if she was crazy to even consider asking him what she was about to. But who better to guide her through the swamp than a man who lived deep within its center?

Besides, he knew Remy, so surely he was all right. Any man would look sort of spooky in this lighting, she rationalized. In the light of day he was probably very ordinary-looking, not spooky at all. This last thought made up her mind. "Mr. Blanchard, I'm planning on going into the swamp while I'm visiting here to take some nature photographs. I could use a guide. Would you be interested?"

He took a step closer to her, bringing with him an earthy, almost herbal scent that was strange, evocative. He stood so near to her she could feel the heat radiating from his body. His gaze seemed to take on a new intensity, and he smiled. But the gesture didn't soften his features as Lindsey had hoped; instead, it only emphasized their harshness. "It's obvious you're new to the area, otherwise you wouldn't ask such a question."

"Why?"

His features seemed to harden, and shadows found the contours of his face as he stared at her. "The last woman who asked me to guide her through the swamp ended up dead."

Lindsey gasped and took another step backward. Before she could ask him anything else, he stepped back, disappearing into the blackness of the night. Moments later the normal sounds resumed and she knew he was gone.

Royce moved through the bog with the familiarity of habit. The swamp didn't frighten him, rather it embraced him like a lover, wrapping its scent around him and filling him with a sense of security.

He slowed his pace, thinking of the woman he'd just left. She'd been pretty, with her curly brown hair and doe-like eyes. A photographer intent on getting pictures of the swamp. He frowned at the thought. She didn't belong here. The swamp didn't like outsiders and neither did he. The past had proven that.

He stopped walking and reached out and touched the rough bark of a cypress tree. The feel was comforting. He listened for a moment to the sound of frogs, the slap of a fish against the water's surface. This place was his and his alone. He understood it, he respected it, he loved it. And he would not share.

Lindsey didn't waste any time going back into the house. She closed the back door and carefully locked it, then flipped off the outside lights. Her heart pounded in an unsteady rhythm. She was spooked, thoroughly, completely unsettled by the strangeness of the scene that had just taken place. Thank God the man hadn't taken her up on her invitation to be her guide. She'd been foolish to even ask. Cindy Mae had often told her that impulsiveness would be the death of her.

She smiled suddenly at her own foolishness. It was only natural that she would feel a little spooked. She was alone in an alien place and her first encounter had been with a man who'd appeared out of the darkness of the night and lived in the swamp. Anyone would be disconcerted under those circumstances.

It would have been nice to have a guide to take her around the swamp, see that she got the best possible photographs of the wonder and mystery. But as she thought of his last statement, she shivered once again.

Shoving thoughts of Royce Blanchard to the back of her head, she went into the kitchen. Her growling stomach reminded her she hadn't eaten since noon, and even then her lunch had been a bad hamburger from a fast-food chain. She just needed something to eat. Everything looked better and brighter on a full stomach.

She opened the refrigerator and frowned in dismay. Other than condiment bottles and a head of withered lettuce, it was disappointingly empty. She checked the freezer compartment, laughing aloud as she saw the note tucked to a carton of caramel ripple ice cream. Caramel ripple was her favorite. She pulled the note from the carton and quickly read it.

Lindsey,
I knew you'd look for the ice cream first. Some things never change! Hope you find everything you need. Afraid we left the fridge rather bare. There's an account set up at Greely's Grocery in Baton Bay. Get whatever you need. Don't forget to baby my plants...they especially like "Over the Rainbow" in the key of C. The air conditioner is most temperamental. Call C. Hawkins if there's a problem. Heal your wounds, dear friend and we'll see you in six weeks!

Cindy

P.S. If Royce Blanchard comes around, stay away from him!

Lindsey stared at the note, reading the last line three times. How like Cindy to issue a warning but give no reason for it.

She set the note on the counter and checked the cabinets, finally finding a box of crackers and a jar of peanut butter. She found a saucer and a butter knife, then carried all the items to the kitchen table.

As she ate, she thought again about Royce Blanchard. Who was he? Why did he live back in the swamp? There had seemed to be a touch of madness in his eyes, an edge of violence tightly restrained.

Was this the reason for Cindy's warning? Was the man crazy? Dangerous? She was intensely grateful that he didn't know Cindy and Remy were gone and she was alone in the house for a month. She frowned suddenly. How many times would he come by looking for Remy before he realized Remy was out of town? How long before Royce Blanchard realized she was here all alone?

With a shake of her head, she buttered another cracker. She was letting her imagination run away with her. What made her think Royce would care one way or the other if she was all alone in the house?

Deciding she really wasn't that hungry, she put the peanut butter and crackers away, placed the saucer and knife in the sink, then headed upstairs to her bedroom.

She ran a tub of hot, bubbly water in the adjoining bathroom, then settled in for a long hot soak.

She closed her eyes, allowing the hot water to work magic on overtense muscles. The past two years, working as John Mitchel's personal secretary and assistant, she hadn't had time to breathe, much less relax and enjoy the indulgence of a bubble bath.

John. Her heart convulsed at thoughts of the man who'd been her boss, then her fiancé. How happy she had been when she'd realized her admiration and love for John was reciprocated. When he'd asked her to be his wife, she'd thought her life was complete.

They had been two weeks away from their wedding when Lindsey had discovered John in bed with Lisa Waring, the new assistant Lindsey had hired for him.

The painful discovery had not only destroyed her dreams for a happily-ever-after with John, but it had also shaken her faith in her own ability to judge other people.

Damn them. Damn them both. She splashed the tub water with her sponge. She brushed droplets of water off her cheeks, unsure if they were tears or merely bathwater. Damn them for stealing away her dreams and leaving her lost, floundering all alone.

She slid farther down in the water and leaned her head back against the cool porcelain of the tub. Yes, this month would be good for her. She'd take this time and indulge herself, and maybe in the process she would discover exactly what it was she wanted to do with the rest of her life.

With a sigh, she decided to get out of the tub. The water had turned tepid and her toes had wrinkled sufficiently. She climbed out and wrapped one of the luxuriously thick towels around her, another one around her shoulder-length hair, then padded into the bedroom.

She pulled on her nightgown and quickly brushed the tangles from her hair, suddenly anxious to go to bed. The bath had relaxed her, making her realize how exhausted she was. The bed, with its crisp white sheets, looked wonderfully inviting.

She turned out the bedside light and moved over to the French doors, pulling back the draperies to allow the moonlight entry.

On impulse, she opened the doors and stepped out onto the small balcony, breathing deeply in the humid air. Her gaze automatically went toward the swamp.

The moonlight was bright, silhouetting the tops of the trees in a ghostly glow. But it was a light not strong enough to permeate the darkness that was the heart of the swamp. A heavy fog had appeared, draping the entire area with a cobweblike grayness. A light breeze stirred, making the entire place move as if it breathed in and out with a life force all its own.

It drew her with its mystical quality, and she couldn't help but think of the man who lived deep within.

Royce Blanchard. Strange how even at this very moment she could almost feel his presence out there. She had the feeling that if she squinted and stared very hard into the center of the swamp where the darkness was most profound, she would see his strange green eyes looking back at her.

With an impatient sigh she whirled around and left the balcony. She was definitely overtired. Still, for her own peace of mind she pulled the draperies tightly closed, blocking out the sight of the foreboding swamp.

Baton Bay was a charming town, as Lindsey discovered early the next morning when she drove in for groceries. The small town was made up of large, well-kept homes with yards carefully manicured and full of blooming flowers. It was obvious Baton Bay was not a tourist town. Main Street boasted no specialty shops selling T-shirts advertising the town or the area. There were no billboards hyping places for family fun or of vacation interest. However, there were the familiar storefronts that spoke of small-town living . . . a drug-store, post office, a grocery store and a general store that instantly caught Lindsey's eye.

It was also obvious to her as she drove slowly down Main Street that it was a place unaccustomed to strangers. People walking down the sidewalks turned and looked at her unfamiliar car, their eyes holding a wariness she found rather amusing. Having grown up in a tiny Kansas community, Lindsey recognized the wariness as a natural outcropping of a small, secluded town.

She found Greely's Groceries with no problems—it was a small store smack-dab in the center of Main. She parked out front and went inside, instantly charmed by the place. Besides the rows of foodstuffs, at the front of the store were several chairs, a table with newspapers scattered about and a coffeemaker perking fresh-ground coffee. It was obvious Greely's Groceries was not only the place to buy the necessities, but also where to go for the latest round of gossip.

Two old men already sat there, arguing about the weather and whether it would be a wetter year than usual.

As Lindsey got a shopping basket and began trekking up and down the aisles, the men's voices rose and fell, sometimes interrupted by the female tones of the old woman who'd been standing at the register.

It took Lindsey only a few minutes to get what she needed, then she pushed her basket up to the register.

"Morning," the old woman greeted her, beginning to ring up the items.

"Good morning," Lindsey returned pleasantly.

"You're new around here." It was a statement rather than a question.

"I'm just visiting at the Clairbournes'."

The old woman's blue eyes lit up and a smile creased her wrinkled face. "Ah, you must be Lindsey. Cindy Mae told us you were going to be watching the house for them while they are gallivanting around Europe. I'm Marge Greely." Marge stopped ringing up the groceries and stuck her hand out to Lindsey. "Cindy told us you were college roommates," Marge continued as she released Lindsey's hand. "Said you were a picture-taking nut . . . her words, not mine."

Lindsey laughed. "Yes, I do a little photography, mostly as a hobby."

"Baton Bay has a lot of pretty places to take pictures of. Be sure and see the flower gardens in the park. The garden club puts a lot of energy into those gardens."

"Actually, I'm thinking about putting together a book of pictures from the swamp."

A frown tugged Marge's smile downward. "Don't you be going too far into that swamp. It's the devil's playground."

"What do you mean?" Lindsey looked at the old woman curiously.

Marge looked around the store, as if wanting to make sure nobody heard what she was about to say. She leaned toward Lindsey, her pale blue eyes wide. "Things go on in that place that have nothing to do with God's handiwork. Evil lives in that swamp. It's not safe for you to wander around in there."

"I asked Royce Blanchard if he would be willing to guide me through it," Lindsey explained.

The old woman gasped and crossed herself, and Lindsey jumped as one of the old men dropped his coffee cup, the porcelain shattering against the floor.

"Damn Sam," the old man muttered, grabbing several napkins and wiping at his lap where the coffee had spilled. As he swiped off his pants, he shot a furtive look at Lindsey.

"Don't even say his name in this place," Marge exclaimed, her gaze again darting around the store. Her wrinkled face had lost all its natural color.

"Why? What's the matter with him?" Lindsey's heart pounded rapidly in her chest as she saw the stark terror that lit Marge's eyes, felt the fear of the two men who stared at her wordlessly.

"Nothing. There's absolutely nothing wrong with him." Marge's features closed in, her tone holding a note of finality.

"But—"

"Your total is $32.87," Marge interrupted. "Cindy Mae told me to put it on their account."

Lindsey watched as the old woman sacked the groceries, her mouth compressed in a tight frown. The two men silently watched, their faces reflecting the closed expression on Marge's.

Lindsey had a feeling she would get no answers here. It was obvious there was something about Royce Blanchard that had them frightened. Their fear was contagious as Lindsey felt an answering shimmer in the pit of her stomach. What was it about the man that even the mention of his name caused such fright?

From the grocery store, she went to the post office, unable to shake the questions that plagued her mind. What was it about Royce that had three grown people afraid to even mention his name? They had been like children, afraid that by speaking of the bogeyman, it would somehow make him real.

She went into the post office, a small building with walls of P.O. boxes, and a single woman employee behind a tiny counter. Lindsey quickly introduced herself to the woman and explained that she would be staying at the Clairbourne place for the next month and would like to have any mail addressed to her delivered there.

"You'll like it here," said the woman, who wore a name tag that read Verla Sue Watkins. Her blond curls bounced as she got out the appropriate forms for Lindsey to fill out. "It takes a while for the people to really warm up to you, but mostly it's a great place."

"How long have you lived here?" Lindsey asked curiously.

"Five years." She laughed. "But unless you're born here, you're never really considered part of the town. Mostly the people are a nice bunch, but quirky."

Lindsey sensed she had found a source of information that would be invaluable. Perhaps the talkative Verla could fill in some of the blanks about the mysterious Royce Blanchard.

She quickly wrote out the required forms, then smiled in friendliness. "You must know everyone in town if you've lived here five years," she commented.

"Working here in the post office is like having a direct link to all the gossip around," Verla said. She leaned forward with a naughty grin. "I could write a book on all the dirt I've heard about the people of Baton Bay." She laughed good-naturedly. "'Course, I'd be tarred and feathered and driven out of town on a rail." She shook her head, allowing her blond curls to swirl out from around her plump face. "Anyone in particular you want to know about?"

"Do you know Royce Blanchard?" Lindsey asked nonchalantly.

Verla's eyes opened wider, and she paused a moment before answering. "You mean Swamp Man?

That's what everyone around here calls him." She picked nervously at a cuticle, then continued. "Nobody really knows Royce Blanchard, but I can tell you what I've heard about him. They say his mother was a swamp witch and his father was the devil himself." She paused a moment, her voice lowering as she went on. "About a year ago he killed a woman."

"Who?" Lindsey's mouth was suddenly dry as she thought of those moments she'd spent alone in the dark with the man.

"Some scientist woman from back East. She came out here about two years ago to study the gators. She went into the swamp and nobody saw her again. Then about a year ago I heard she was dead, that the Swamp Man killed her. Some say he fed her body to the gators. Others say he kept her body and turned her into a zombie who walks the swamp at night." Verla shook her head. "I also heard the woman had a baby, and he killed it, too. They say when the wind blows through the swamp you can hear the ghost cries of that murdered little baby."

"Why isn't he in jail?" Lindsey asked incredulously.

Verla shrugged. "No hard evidence, I guess. Besides, would you go into that swamp to arrest him?"

Lindsey worked to control an involuntary shiver. "Do you believe all the stories about him?" she asked, her voice a low whisper.

Verla shrugged again. "Have you ever seen Royce?" Lindsey nodded and Verla continued. "He's as handsome as Satan himself, you know what I'm talking about... but there's something about him that's scary... a look in his eyes.... I think he's crazy. He'd have to be crazy to live in his little shanty back in the swamp." She shivered suddenly and wrapped her arms around her shoulders. "I look at it this way—where there's smoke, there's fire. And concerning Royce Blanchard, there's plenty of smoke."

Moments later as she drove back to Cindy's house, Verla's words whirled around in Lindsey's head. Murder, zombies, ghost babies... the whole story seemed preposterous, but it was difficult to discount the genuine fear she had seen in everyone's eyes when they spoke of him. And as Lindsey remembered the strange glitter in Royce's compelling green eyes, none of it seemed quite so outrageous.

CHAPTER TWO

For the next three days Lindsey avoided going into the swamp, put off by the strange stories she'd heard in town about the man who lived there.

In the early mornings she watched the sun rise, breaking over the tops of the trees, spilling its golden light to the earth. She took several camera shots from the balcony but knew she wouldn't be satisfied until she got closer to the heart of the place.

She spent the days puttering around the house, singing to Cindy Mae's plants and thumbing through the variety of magazines Cindy subscribed to. But always, no matter what she was doing, her thoughts were on the marshland behind the house.

Each night before nightfall she took a cup of coffee with her back up to the balcony. For it was at this time that the swamp called to her, its magnetic pull an almost overwhelming command. She watched the sunset turn the tops of the cypress trees to fire, making their orange and flame colors a fascinating contradiction to the darkness that expanded outward from the center of the swamp. It was from the dark heart of the swamp that she felt a compelling force that spoke to her, a pulse beat that echoed in her veins.

In the darkness, she would stand on the balcony, staring at the junglelike area, fighting against the desire it called up in her. She could almost imagine that the breeze spoke her name as it blew through the tangled vegetation, whispered among the tops of the trees.

By midafternoon of her fourth day, she decided she was being foolish in avoiding the very place where she wanted so desperately to go. After all, it was a big area—the odds were good that she wouldn't even see Royce Blanchard.

Slinging her camera around her neck, she took off walking across the back yard, her pulse quickening as she approached the swamp. As her feet left the manicured grass, they carried her onto a low-lying patch of ground that sucked at her tennis shoes with moistness. Surrounding her were bursts of flowers, strange ones she'd never seen before and couldn't name.

She stood motionless, admiring the beauty of the blossoms, then realized a strange noise surrounded her . . . a constant sound that rose and fell like musical notes on a page. Frogs, thousands of frogs, she realized, feeling some relief in identifying the mélange of sound.

Her camera clicked and whirled as she captured on film the beauty of her surroundings. A great blue heron stood on a dead, fallen tree, its image captured by her on film. Beneath her feet sphagnum moss crept inexorably in every direction like a thick, tangled carpet. Berries adorned many of the bushes and thickets, looking lush in shades of red and purple.

As she walked farther, the beauty disappeared, swallowed up by the more sinister elements of the swamp. The ground beneath her feet turned to loose, wet peat that trembled ominously with every step she took. The cypress now enveloped her, creating an illusion of her being inside something . . . like a huge, dark cave. She passed large ponds of dark water, the pungent scent of decaying vegetation prevalent. Knobby cypress knees protruded from the water, contorted and weird-looking, making her feel like she had entered a landscape from a science-fiction novel.

She paused to put a fresh roll of film into the camera, wanting to capture the gloom, the wildness, the mystery of the area. She focused the lens on a log in the water of a nearby pool. Perched atop the log was a beautiful red-and-gray bird. Lindsey carefully aimed. With a sudden thrashing of water, the "log" became an alligator, his huge jaws snapping shut on the little bird. In the blink of an eye the bird disappeared into the horrendous mouth and the alligator once again lay quiet, half-submerged in the water.

Suddenly, Lindsey was frightened by the place that surrounded her. Where before she had seen beauty, she was now struck with the fear of the unknown. The swamp had transformed to a savage and menacing presence where rules of civility no longer applied. Here there existed only the stark essentials of survival.

She felt an overwhelming desire to get out, go back to the familiarity of Cindy's yard. She secured her camera back in the case that hung from a strap around her neck, then turned to retrace her steps. She hadn't thought about the creatures who lived in the swamp . . . alligators, snakes—this place was home to a variety of animals she didn't particularly want to encounter.

After walking for a few minutes, she realized she wasn't going the way she had come. She stopped, looking around in confusion, searching for some familiar landmark, but there were none. The trees all looked alike, the junglelike surroundings dense in every direction.

She gazed upward, noting the waning light that spoke of day's death. Staring at her watch, she felt the first tickle of fear whispering in the pit of her stomach. It would be getting dark soon and her heart clutched convulsively at the thought of being lost out here at night.

She moved more quickly in the direction she thought was right, fighting down a sickening sense of panic. The swamp had now taken on the dimension of an enemy to be outrun. The thickets seemed to jump out at her, scratching at her with thorny fingernails. The vines grabbed at her ankles, attempting to trip her. The ground beneath her sucked at her feet, as if trying to drag her down and hold her in its mulchlike consistency. The Spanish moss reached down from where it hung above her, trying to drape her in its gray shroud. She ducked, stifling a small scream. She had a feeling that if the moss captured her it would enshrine her forever as it had so many of the cypress trees.

Lindsey ran blindly, her panic at full throttle. She had to get out of this place. She had to escape. She emitted a cry as her foot caught on a root and she stumbled to the ground, the air whooshing out of her as if from a punctured balloon. She lay for a moment, stunned, gasping in an attempt to take in air. As she lay there, she realized the ever-present noise of the swamp had silenced. It was just as it had been on the night she'd first met him...the quiet, so profound and deep. She felt his presence not only in the silence, but in her heart, which pounded in an uneasy rhythm. She sat up and looked around, unsurprised when she saw him.

He stood beside an ancient cypress, its gnarled base leaning toward him as if in an embrace. He was shirtless, wearing only a pair of gray jeans and sturdy work boots. He was all the colors of the swamp...his sunbronzed skin a bark brown, his eyes the hues of a primeval forest. His hair was the darkness of mystery. He didn't look to be so much *from* the swamp as *of* the swamp.

Once again she felt her breathing grow labored as he walked over to where she sat. As he towered over her he looked like a menacing warlock, come to steal her soul.

She scrambled to her feet and backed away, unsure what she feared more, the threat of darkness in the swamp or the man who stood before her.

"I...I'm lost." She rubbed her hands nervously down the sides of her jeans, taking another step back from him.

He said nothing, merely looked at her. And in the depths of his green eyes she once again saw a touch of madness, one that made her believe there could be some truth to the rumors she'd heard.

"Uh...if you could just point me in the right direction...."

"It will be dark soon," he said as if he hadn't heard her request. He breathed deeply, seeming to gain sustenance from the pungent air. He looked around, then redirected his gaze onto her. "The swamp comes alive at night."

Already evening shadows found the hollows of his face, emphasizing the harsh lines. Lindsey felt her fear expanding, growing within her like an alien entity. She was paralyzed with it, afraid of him, afraid of the swamp. Her brain urged her to run, but her body refused to obey the command. Besides, in which direction would she run? She stared at him wordlessly, for a moment unable to speak as her fear clogged her throat.

"Sometimes people come into the swamp and they are never seen again." His voice was ominously soft, and she couldn't tell if his words were meant to be a warning or a threat. He took another step toward her, the strange glimmer in his eyes hypnotizing... terrifying. "I guess I'd better get you out of here before something bad happens to you." He turned and started to walk off. "Come on." He didn't wait for her to reply, instead stalking into the lengthening twilight.

Lindsey hesitated, unsure what to do. He scared her, but she was hopelessly lost and on her own would probably never make it out of the swamp. At the moment, Royce seemed the lesser of two evils, but not less enough for her to feel comforted. Still, as he disappeared into the thick underbrush, she hurried after him, afraid of being left on her own.

She followed behind him, maintaining a healthy distance. He moved with the agility and grace of a wild animal, his brown back muscles rippling with a strength both tantalizing and intimidating.

The stories she'd heard about him tumbled through her head, as dark as the shadows stealing stealthily through the swamp. Murdered women, zombies, ghost babies . . . a mother who was a witch and a father who was the devil. Who was this Royce Blanchard? And how much of the stories they whispered about him was true?

As he turned and looked back at her, his face held a tormented intensity, and in that moment Lindsey believed each and every story she'd heard about him.

Her footsteps slowed as she studied the surroundings. Nothing looked even vaguely familiar. A blackened tree stump stood off to the left, testimony to a fire at one time or another. Surely she would remember if she'd passed the black skeleton before.

Was he taking her to safety or leading her to his lair? She had a feeling her odds of survival would be greater against the swamp than with the brute strength of his shoulders and the madness in his eyes.

She had just about decided to veer away from him, trust the instincts that said she should run, when she saw him break through the thicket and onto Cindy's manicured grounds.

She quickly followed, sighing in relief. The sigh caught in her throat as he suddenly whirled around, grabbed her by the shoulders and pulled her roughly against the hard length of his body.

"We don't like outsiders. The swamp and I like to be left alone," he said, his breath hot and wild against her face.

She felt a trembling and wasn't sure if it came from her own fear or if it was him shaking with an effort to control the rage she saw in his eyes.

"You should listen to what they say about me, Lindsey. You should believe and be very afraid."

Lindsey was intensely aware of his body pressed against her own. His chest was firmly muscled, unyielding against the soft fullness of her breasts. His flesh was hot, as if fevered by the madness that muddled his eyes. His arms bulged with a powerful strength, and as one hand moved from her shoulder to encircle her neck, Lindsey wondered if it had been the strength of his hands that had killed the female scientist.

Now she knew the trembling was her own. Her mind shut off and her body responded to him with gut-wrenching terror. Her breath came in painful pants as a fist of cold fear wrenched deep in her stomach.

The hand around the base of her neck did not exert pressure, but the horror of its threatening presence there made breathing difficult.

"Don't come back into the swamp. Stay away from it and stay away from me." His eyes burned into hers. "Because the next time there's no guarantee you'll get out."

He released her as suddenly as he'd grabbed her, causing her to stumble away from him with a gasp.

She turned and ran, not stopping until she'd reached the edge of the pool. She paused there, taking deep gulps of air, trying to stop the trembling of her insides.

She believed she'd just felt the breath of death on her face and for some reason had been granted a reprieve. Crazy...the man was truly crazy. She'd seen it in his eyes, felt it in his hand as it had touched her skin.

She turned and looked back at the swamp. He was still there, standing at the edge, blending in with his surroundings like a chameleon coloring itself for protection. For a long moment they stared at each other, and even from this distance his gaze was as powerful as a touch on the shoulder. As she watched, he stepped back, disappearing, becoming part of the swamp once again.

Lindsey walked quickly toward Cindy's house, needing the safety, the security of the locked doors. She went inside and leaned against the back door, trying to calm her heartbeat, which still raced with fear. A shuddering sigh raced through her, catching in her throat as a sudden thought pierced her brain. He'd known her name. How in the hell had he known her name?

Royce's rage was a living, breathing thing as he made his way back to the cabin that was home. He trembled with the force of his emotion. How dare she come into his swamp? How dare she violate what was his?

Lindsey Witherspoon. He'd learned her name today on one of his rare trips into town. Her name now fluttered through his head, conjuring up her physical features in his mind. She was a beauty all right, all that soft, curly hair and those eyes that had widened with terror. He grunted in satisfaction as he remembered that look of terror. She'd been afraid. Good. He wanted her to be afraid.

He'd thought he'd conquered the need. He'd believed he'd gained control of the demons that drove him. But like a mutant monster, the need was once again growing inside of him, expanding out of control. And God help him if he let it go. God help her....

The air-conditioning wasn't working. Lindsey awoke in the middle of the night, the sheets twisted around her like confining arms. Her body was covered with a fine sheen of perspiration, and at first she thought it was a result of the nightmares that had plagued her sleep. Strange dreams of Royce and the swamp, ones that both frightened and confused her. She'd been running through the swamp, the vegetation alive and clutching at her, trying to impede her progress with thorny fingers and grabbing limbs.

Her heart still pounded with the memory of the dreams, the fear that had been her companion as she raced through the brush, screaming his name as she ran. The strange thing was, she'd had the distinct impression that in the dream she'd been running into the swamp rather than away from it. Bizarre . . . it had all been very bizarre.

She untangled her legs from the twisted sheets and got out of bed, immediately realizing that the room was hot and the air conditioner ominously silent.

The memory of her dream followed her as she moved down the large stairway to where the thermostat hung on the wall. She moved the lever down as low as it would go and waited for the fan to kick on and send out cooling waves of air.

As she waited, she leaned back against the wall and closed her eyes, replaying the unsettling dream she'd just experienced.

Surely it had been prompted by the encounter with Royce. Surely it had merely been her subconscious trying to work through the terror of his hand around her neck, the warning in his voice, the touch of dementia in his eyes. There was no getting around it. He had soundly scared her, and surely that was what had caused the nightmares.

Still, none of this explained why when she'd awakened she'd been left with the distinct impression that she'd been running into the swamp, toward the madness and the danger of Royce Blanchard.

And what frightened her even more was the aware-
ness that for a single, quick-silver moment, as she'd
been pulled against the hardness of his body, as she'd
felt the heat of his skin, a primitive, wild desire had
surged within her. It had appeared for only a moment, quickly stifled by the panic and fear he'd pro-
voked.

She pushed herself away from the wall with a sigh
of disgust. Apparently this heat was turning her brain
to mush.

She went into the kitchen and put a teakettle of water on to boil. Maybe a hot cup of tea would relax her
enough to find sleep once again despite the sultry, oppressive heat.

After two cups of the hot brew, she went back upstairs. She crawled back into bed, still unsettled, and
spent the rest of the night tossing and turning in rest-
lessness.

At seven-thirty the next morning she called C.
Hawkins and made arrangements for him to come as
soon as possible to fix the temperamental air conditioner.

At precisely eight o'clock, a battered pickup truck
pulled up out front and Charley Hawkins introduced
himself. He was a middle-aged man who chattered af-
fably as Lindsey accompanied him around to the back
of the house where the cooling unit sat on a concrete
slab.

"I've told Remy a dozen times to junk this old
clunker and put in a new one," Charley exclaimed as
he tinkered with the air-conditioning unit. "'Course

Remy, he's a stubborn one. It's that Cajun blood in him.''

"Do you think you can fix it?" Lindsey asked anxiously, not enjoying the thought of a six-week stay without the luxury of a cool house.

"I think the old girl still has a little life left in her," he replied, pulling a wrench out of the huge tool chest he'd brought with him. "I heard in town you were staying out here. How do you like our town?"

"From what I've seen of it, it seems really nice," Lindsey answered.

"'Course, it's not much of a place to be if you have to work for a living. Other than the few stores, there isn't much way to make a living in Baton Bay."

"What does everyone do?" Lindsey asked curiously.

"Most folks have jobs in Cypress Corners. It's about an hour drive from here. It's a bigger town, got a couple factories and lots of businesses."

Lindsey nodded, raising her face to the warmth of the early morning sun. In the brightness of day, her dreams and the unease of the night before seemed foolish. She was letting her imagination and the gloomy atmosphere of the nearby swamp get to her.

She turned and looked at the swamp. The sunshine painted the tops of the trees, but the core of the place remained dark, as if something within it had the power to repel the light. She shivered and redirected her attention back to Charley.

She rubbed her temples with the tips of her fingers, hoping to ease the ache that had begun to pound there.

She always got a headache when she'd had too little sleep. And last night had definitely been a sleepless night.

"There, I think that should hold it for a while," Charley said, giving the screws on the metal cover a final twist. He stood up and grinned at her. "Being this close to the swamp you need a good air conditioner so you don't have to keep your windows open for air. Don't want no swamp boogers creeping into open windows." His gaze shot to the nearby bog and his smile wavered slightly.

"Certainly not," Lindsey agreed, feeling her headache expanding across the front of her forehead.

After Charley left, Lindsey rummaged around in the main bathroom cabinet until she found a bottle of aspirin. Swallowing two, she went back into the living room and stretched out on the sofa.

John... As always when she had a moment's solitude, her thoughts went to him and all she'd lost. She'd been so blithely happy making the wedding plans and preparing for their future together. Looking back now she couldn't figure out when John's love for her had died. But on the day she'd walked into his apartment and discovered him in bed with Lisa, Lindsey knew it didn't matter that he'd stopped loving her. The love she'd had for him crumbled and died, leaving behind only a cold, empty echoing in her heart.

The heartache had dissipated over the last couple of weeks. She found a certain amount of comfort in the fact that she'd been spared a marriage to a man who was obviously wrong for her.

Still, she mourned the loss of the future she'd envisioned, a loving husband and babies. She'd wanted babies, lots of them. Raised as an only child with parents who were old when she was born, Lindsey had always dreamed of marrying and filling a house with kids. She'd wanted that with a passion, but now it was all gone.

Headache relieved and tired of muddling around in her unhappy past, she got up, deciding she'd take a trip into town. She had the roll of film from the day before that she wanted to take in and get developed.

A half hour later, Lindsey pulled her car into a parking place on Main Street, excited as she saw a sign in the drugstore window advertising one-hour developing.

Minutes later she came out of the store, pleased that she'd have her pictures back within the hour. She'd take her time and wander in and out of the stores. Maybe the mundane act of window-shopping would chase away the last, lingering bit of unease she'd felt since awakening from her restless sleep.

It seemed to do the trick. As she wandered in and out of the stores, she felt her spirits lifting. If the photos were good, she'd put together a portfolio and send it off to a publisher she'd chosen who was known for printing nature books. If they liked the pictures, it could be the beginning of a new career for her. Of course, she could always go back to another secretarial position if things didn't work out with her photography.

In the general store she bought a tiny, exquisite crystal duck for Cindy. A thank-you gift for letting her stay in their home while they were gone. She was pleased with the purchase, knowing her friend had always been partial to ducks of all shapes and sizes.

Then, looking at her watch, she realized it was almost time for her pictures to be ready. She walked down the sidewalk, humming a cheery nonsensical tune beneath her breath. The shadows that had marked the past two days were gone, banished by the joy of finding the gift for Cindy and the anticipation of seeing her photos.

She jumped as a hand touched her shoulder from behind. She turned to see an old woman dressed in black, her waist-length white hair a startling contrast. The woman's face was wrinkled with time's passage, but displayed a proud strength that was arresting. "I hold the secrets of your future." Her voice was low, husky. Her dark eyes bore into Lindsey's intensely.

"I beg your pardon?" Lindsey stepped back from the woman in surprise.

The old woman reached out and plucked at Lindsey's sleeve insistently. "Come, let me tell you what fate holds in store for you." She gestured to the storefront behind her. Painted on the pane of glass were the words Fortunes by Madame Obediah. "Come inside, let me gaze into your future and tell you what I see. Madame Obediah sees all the future holds," the woman urged.

Why not? Lindsey thought with amusement. If nothing else it would make a good story to tell when she returned to Washington, D.C. With a slight nod of her head, she allowed the old woman to lead her inside.

After the brilliant sunshine, it took Lindsey's eyes several moments to adjust to the darkness of the room. Heavy dark curtains at the window blocked out any seepage of sun into the room.

It was a small area, the walls adorned with shelves of curious bottles and jars. The air was heavy with the pungent odor of incense and herbs, and other indefinable smells that were slightly unpleasant.

"Please, sit down." Madame Obediah motioned her to a chair at the table where two candles flickered, causing furtive shadow-dancers to appear on the walls.

Lindsey slid into the chair, unable to suppress a small grin. What would it be? Tea leaves? Tarot cards? Or would Madame Obediah tell her future by looking at the lines in her palms? The bumps on her head? At least she'd go home with a great story to tell at some of the boring D.C. cocktail parties she occasionally attended.

Lindsey had never believed in this kind of nonsense, but it seemed fitting that at this juncture in her life she enjoy the novelty of having her future told. Perhaps she'd learn something new about herself.

She watched with interest as the old woman took a velvet pouch off the shelf and set it on the table. With a flourish of her hands, she untied the top of the pouch and poured the contents out onto the tabletop.

Lindsey's smile faded and she swallowed a gasp as she saw what the bag had contained. Bones...polished to a high shine, but bones nevertheless.

Madame Obediah gathered them in her hands then dropped them, like a child beginning a game of pickup sticks. She stared at Lindsey expectantly, making Lindsey realize she wanted her to drop the bones in the same manner.

Trying to hide her grimace of distaste, Lindsey gingerly gathered the polished pieces in one hand, repulsed by how cold they were to her touch. She released them quickly, stifling a shudder as they rattled against the tabletop. Rattling bones... How utterly disgusting, Lindsey thought.

Madame Obediah stared at them for a long moment, then looked up at Lindsey. "You've had a recent heartbreak."

Lindsey's smile returned, and she nodded in amusement. That was pretty benign. Nine out of ten women who came in here to get their fortunes told were probably suffering from a recent heartbreak. With that kind of general statement the odds were definitely in Madame Obediah's favor.

Madame Obediah looked down at the pieces once again, then back at Lindsey, and there was something in her dark eyes that sent a chill through Lindsey.

"Go home. You don't belong here." The old woman allowed her head to loll forward, and when she raised it again her eyes were glazed and unfocused. She muttered several words in a language Lindsey didn't recognize.

"What?" Lindsey stared at the woman. "What's wrong? What do you see?"

Madame Obediah shook her head, emitting a guttural moan that sent a sense of horror through Lindsey. The old woman began a loud keening noise, her head rolling around as if her spine had snapped.

"Please . . ." Lindsey's voice trembled. "Please tell me what you see." She sat forward, eager yet dreading what the woman would say.

"You are in terrible danger here." The words shot out of the woman harshly. "It surrounds you like a shroud."

The cloying incense made Lindsey's head reel and her heart pound in a rapid tattoo. She felt suddenly disoriented, as if she teetered on the brink of a black hole. "What? What surrounds me?" Lindsey whispered, the terror in the old woman's eyes feeding the fear growing in her.

"The veil of death," Madame Obediah shouted, the words making the hair on the back of Lindsey's neck stand straight out.

Lindsey jumped up, unmindful of the wooden chair that crashed to the floor behind her. She felt dizzy, suffocated, and needed to get out.

"Your soul is in jeopardy. You must leave this place. . . . Leave!"

Madame Obediah's words chased Lindsey out of the store, back into the sanity of the sunshine.

CHAPTER THREE

She's just a silly old woman, Lindsey told herself as she stood on the sidewalk outside, trying to swallow the lump of fear that still lodged in her throat.

The old woman probably got her kicks by scaring the few tourists and visitors who came into town. Lindsey didn't believe any of the superstitious nonsense. Veil of death, indeed, she scoffed, raising her face to the welcome warmth of the sun.

Breathing deeply of the jasmine-scented air, she felt her inner trembling passing as the horror began to recede. It was all just a bunch of foolishness, she told herself firmly.

After getting her envelope of pictures she paused, deciding to cross the street and go into the Lazy Day Café.

Maybe a cup of coffee would settle her nerves enough so that she would feel more like driving back to Cindy's place. At the moment, her anxiety was still too keen for her to want to return to Cindy's house where she would be all alone.

The air in the café was rich with the scent of frying fish and Cajun spices. She found a certain comfort in the normal sounds of silverware clinking and people laughing.

She slid into a booth near the back and ordered a cup of coffee, looking around the room, needing to reassure herself that everything was okay...normal.

She didn't open up her envelope of photos, not wanting her first view of them to be tainted by the taste of fear that still lingered in her mouth.

She smiled as the waitress brought her a steaming cup of thick chicory brew. She took a tentative sip, hoping the heat of the drink would warm the cold knot that still sat in her stomach.

Perhaps Madame Obediah's words wouldn't have hit so hard if Lindsey hadn't felt so threatened by her encounter with Royce in the swamp. If she hadn't already felt the hint of danger surrounding her when she'd met up with him, the old woman's words would have fallen on deaf ears.

Dammit, the whole thing not only frightened her, but it also made her angry. John had discouraged her interest in photography. Looking back at that relationship with a new objectivity, she now realized how controlling John had been. He'd laughed indulgently when she'd first told him she'd like to be a professional photographer. He'd patronized her, talked about her little "hobby," belittled her dreams. And now she had some crazy man from the swamp warning her to stay away, controlling where she could and where she couldn't take pictures. It just didn't seem fair.

She sighed and took another sip of her coffee.

"Lindsey, mind if I join you?"

She looked up to see the plump Verla Sue, the woman from the post office, standing next to her booth. "Sure, have a seat." Lindsey gestured to the seat across from her.

Verla slid in with a friendly smile. "Terrific, I hate eating lunch alone. I only get a half hour, but it's nicer to share it with someone." She raised her hand to the waitress. "Just bring me the usual," she yelled, then smiled once again at Lindsey, her blond curls bobbing as if with a life of their own. "I come in here every day. They have the best catfish in town. Of course, the grease goes right to my hips." She eyed Lindsey jealously. "Bet you don't have that problem. You're as thin as a pickle."

Lindsey laughed, finding Verla's friendly chatter a welcome respite from the darkness of her conversation with Madame Obediah. "I've always been lucky. Cindy Mae used to say I have the metabolism of a racehorse."

"You're lucky all right. I've always had to watch every single thing that goes into my mouth." She patted her thighs. "And most of the time I lose the battle." She paused and looked at Lindsey seriously. "You've been friends with Cindy Mae and Remy a long time?"

"Cindy and I went to college together. I met Remy a year ago when he and Cindy came to visit me in Washington, D.C. We hit it off right away. This is my first visit down here," Lindsey explained.

"They're a real nice couple, although why they'd want to live in that house so close to the swamp is beyond me." Verla shivered. "That place gives me the willies."

Again Lindsey laughed. "Cindy Mae was always the one in college who wanted to go see the latest horror film. If there was a haunted house around, she visited it. If someone knew a ghost story, she wanted to hear it. She's always loved to be scared."

"Not me," Verla exclaimed. "It's one thing to be scared by images on a screen in a movie theater, quite another to be frightened by something that exists right outside your back door. That swamp place is evil."

Lindsey sipped her coffee and smiled reflectively. "A place can't be evil. It's a little scary, but that's because it's dark and mysterious. It's also beautiful in a primitive sort of way." She picked up the envelope of photos she'd pushed to one side. "I was in the swamp yesterday taking some pictures. You want to see them?"

"Sure," Verla agreed enthusiastically, her blue eyes sparkling. "I love to look at pictures."

Lindsey removed the photos and, without looking at them, handed the stack to Verla. She held her breath as Verla silently studied each one in turn. *They're bad,* Lindsey thought in dismay. *That's why she isn't commenting on them. The pictures are horrible.*

"These are ... terrific!" Verla's eyes sparkled with admiration as she looked at each photo a second time.

"You really think so?" Lindsey asked anxiously.

"Really. You're very talented. The play of the light on these flowers, the action of the gator shot ... you've captured some really great images."

Pride swelled up inside Lindsey as she took the pictures from Verla and studied each one carefully. Yes, they were good. They were better than good. They were great!

"Here you go, Verla," the waitress said, appearing at their table with a platter of blackened catfish, French fries and coleslaw. "You sure you don't want anything, honey?" The waitress eyed Lindsey curiously.

Lindsey shook her head. "No, thanks. I'm fine."

With a shrug the waitress left the table. "You don't know what you're missing," Verla exclaimed, using her fingers to pick up a piece of the crispy fish. "I've never tasted better fish than right here."

"I'm really not that hungry. I just stopped in here for a cup of coffee to sort of calm my nerves," Lindsey exclaimed. She paused a moment, then continued. "I had my fortune read this morning by Madame Obediah."

Verla laughed. "How much did the old coot take you for?" At Lindsey's blank look, Verla continued. "How much did she charge you?"

"She didn't charge me anything," Lindsey answered. Now that she thought about it, that was rather strange.

Verla frowned. "Hmm, usually Madame Obediah is mute until you cross her palm with a twenty-dollar bill." Her frown disappeared and she grinned. "So, what did she tell you? Let me guess..." Verla closed her eyes and tilted her head sideways as if she were communicating with the other world. "You have recently been hurt by a man." She popped one eye open and looked at Lindsey, then closed it again and continued. "Soon you will meet a tall, dark, handsome man who will make you forget all your previous heartaches."

Lindsey laughed. "You've got it pretty close except she didn't offer me any hope of a tall, dark, handsome man coming into my life to ease my pained heart."

Verla's grin widened and she shook her head ruefully. "That woman really should be arrested. Who knows what she sells out of that place besides fortunes. Did you see all those weird bottles and jars? Probably toad lips and lizard tails." Verla paused to pop another piece of fish into her mouth. "The sheriff gets complaints about her all the time, but he says anyone who's dumb enough to go into her store deserves to get their money taken."

"She gave quite a convincing performance," Lindsey observed, remembering the chills that had danced up her spine as she'd sat across from the old woman.

"Supposedly she's into voodoo. Her ancestors were all swamp people, but she's lived in town for as long as anyone can remember." Verla looked at Lindsey curiously. "So, what else did she tell you?"

"Oh, nothing really. Just a bunch of nonsense." Lindsey picked up her coffee cup and took another sip, wanting nothing but to forget the old woman's words.

* * *

Just a bunch of nonsense, Lindsey repeated to herself moments later as she drove back to Cindy Mae's place. Madame Obediah probably gave the same spine-tingling spiel to everyone who came into her shop. Lindsey would be crazy to believe it was anything other than that. Imagine a grown woman being spooked by the performance of a fortune-teller. She refused to think about the foolishness any longer.

She rolled down the car window, allowing in the fragrant, sultry air. There was something sensually pleasing about the atmosphere here. Thick, languid, with an overwhelming floral scent, the air evoked images of moonlight and passion. It was too bad she had nobody to share it all with.

Again she thought of that brief moment when she'd felt Royce Blanchard's body pressed so tightly against her own. Perhaps it really hadn't been desire that had stirred deep within her. Maybe it had just been emotions heightened by fear. Yes, that was it. She'd mistaken the coursing adrenaline as desire.

With this straight in her mind, her thoughts moved onward, to the swamp and Royce's warning for her to stay away. After seeing the photographs she'd taken, she knew there was no way she was going to avoid the swamp. She'd be damned if she'd let a man, even a crazy swamp-dweller, deter her from her work.

She was going to enter the swamp again, only this time she would be wiser. She'd take precautions.

It was almost three o'clock in the afternoon when she decided to brave the swamp again. This time, she was prepared—she had a pocketful of bright yellow ribbons and a can of Mace. "Swamp boogers beware," she muttered bravely as she advanced into its depths.

As she walked, she slipped the telephoto lens onto her camera. She hadn't used the special lens the day before. She'd saved to buy it for nearly a month, and today would be the first time she tried it. She was excited at the prospect, knowing the expensive lens would get her better, clearer shots than she'd ever taken.

She paused every few steps to tie a ribbon on a low tree limb or a bush, knowing they would serve as bright beacons and guide her back to where she'd entered the bog.

Within minutes she was once again caught up in the mystery and wonder of the swamplands. The sun peeked through, a glaring yellow eye shining its warmth but not banishing the coolness of the shadowed underbrush. She passed a slow-moving, shallow creek, its water the color of weak coffee.

Her camera caught it all, the egrets flying overhead, clots of floating plants which provided transportation for little leopard frogs.

The darker elements of the swamp were also present. A four-foot-long black snake rattled its tail and sped away from her footsteps. A large lizard hung from a tree branch, its long tongue darting out to capture some of the mosquitoes that swarmed the area. An alligator peered at her from behind a bed of water lilies.

She paused a moment, swiping at a trickle of perspiration that edged down the side of her face. She sat down on a fallen log, careful to avoid the gray-and-red lichen that clung to the bark.

The swamp breathed around her. She could hear the subtle movement of its life, a soft breeze caressing her face like a sigh. It was easy to see why Royce had spoken of the swamp as if it was a person. It had an aura, a character all its own. And she knew with certainty that although at the moment it was a benign personification, exhibiting a calm, beautiful nature, it could transform in the blink of an eye and become a raging, horrifying witch.

She looked at her wristwatch, noting that it was nearly five o'clock. Time to get back to the house. She'd been lucky so far. She hadn't seen a sign of Royce. No sense in pushing that luck. She stood up and placed her camera and the expensive lens in her bag, then, checking to make sure the can of Mace was still tucked in her back pocket, she started retracing her steps, searching for the bright ribbons she'd used to mark her way.

She found the first one. Not far away, she found the second one. There the trail ended. There was no sign of another yellow ribbon. She turned in a circle, looking for a flash of bright color. They had to be here. She'd tied them securely and at regular intervals. She'd been very careful, knowing they would guide her back to safety. She frowned and looked again. They couldn't have just disappeared into thin air.

"Looking for these?"

She jumped, startled by his voice. As always, he seemed to materialize out of nowhere, appearing before her like a ghostly wraith. He held out his hand, which was clenched into a fist, the yellow ribbons spilling out like snakes escaping a basket.

She touched the can of Mace in her back pocket, reassured by its presence. "I was using those to find my way back." She was pleased that her voice didn't tremble. There was no audible sign of the tremor that raced through her at his appearance.

"You were told not to come back here." His voice was flat, emotionless, but his eyes smoldered with a fervency that sparked apprehension in her. "You were warned."

She raised her chin, refusing to show him the anxiety that caused her heart to thud erratically in her chest. "You don't own the swamp, Mr. Blanchard."

He tilted his head to the side, looking at her as if she were a mutated form of plant life he'd never seen before. "True," he agreed, "but I understand her. I know her nuances, her moods. I respect her strengths and allow her weaknesses."

"You love it," Lindsey said softly.

He shrugged his powerful shoulders. "It's who I am." He took several steps toward her, bringing with him the scent of the bayou, wet heat and mysterious darkness. His eyes were now as dark and enigmatic as the motionless waters of the swamp ponds. "You are a foolish woman, Lindsey Witherspoon."

"No, merely stubborn. I don't like to be told where I can go and where I can't." Lindsey once again reached behind her and placed her hand on the can of Mace, ready to whip it out and use it if necessary.

"Sometimes stubbornness can get people hurt."

He now stood close enough to her that she could see the pulse that ticked in his jaw, a small mole that decorated the side of his neck, a jagged scar that began just below his navel and disappeared into the low-slung jeans. Did the man never wear a shirt?

"You've made it difficult for me to get back home, and Cindy and Remy will be wondering where I am," she bluffed anxiously.

He smiled, a hard, cold gesture that did nothing to relieve the harsh lines of his face. "That's interesting. It must be very difficult for Cindy and Remy to keep tabs on you while they're traveling in Europe."

So he knew. He knew that she was all alone in the house. The thought sent another shiver through her. As he took another step toward her, Lindsey pulled the Mace from her back pocket and pointed it at his face.

His smile deepened, his eyes glittering with challenge. "Be careful, Lindsey. If you spray that at me, the only thing you're going to accomplish is to make me very angry. And believe me, you don't want to make me angry."

The can of Mace, which had always seemed a civilized, effective weapon back in D.C., now seemed ridiculous and ineffectual. For another long moment she kept the can pointed at his face, torn between the need to protect herself and the fear that by spraying him she might, indeed, merely serve to make him angry. And she believed him. She didn't want to see his rage.

Slowly, reluctantly, she slipped the can back into her pocket. She had no other choice but to trust the instinct that told her if he really wanted to harm her, he'd probably had a dozen opportunities in the past two hours that she'd been wandering around alone.

She faced him with a boldness that masked her faint heart, hoping that her instincts would prove correct. "Since you've removed all my ribbons, I can only assume you intend to lead me out of here."

"Perhaps you assume too much."

"I guess I've always been a cockeyed optimist," Lindsey muttered with false bravado.

For the briefest moment there was a new light in his eyes, as if the sun had found the murky waters of a pond and illuminated the shadows beneath the surface. It was only there a moment, then quickly swallowed by the darkness once again. "Come on, then."

Once again she found herself following the man of the swamp, wondering about the many stories that surrounded him. He was as mysterious as their surroundings, and the rumors she'd heard about him only fed the mystique, deepened her intrigue.

But she was smart enough to know that it was an intrigue she wouldn't pursue. It was an interest that could prove dangerous.

He didn't speak again as he led her through the dark underbrush. His silence lent an additional somber element to the already dark aura he presented.

She had followed behind him for fifteen minutes, fighting through the tangled brush, stepping across wide pools of dank water, when he stopped and turned to her. He pointed to a path that veered off to the left of him. "If you follow this for about a hundred yards, you'll come out by the swimming pool."

Lindsey nodded, moving to brush past him and take the direction he'd indicated. As she moved by, he reached out and grabbed her arm, stopping her in her tracks.

Although his touch was light, it was the expression in his eyes that effectively pinned her motionless, a prisoner of his gaze. His eyes were devoid of shadows, instead their green depths held the torment of a man haunted by demons.

His hand reached up and touched her curls, almost as if he couldn't help himself. For a moment it was as if he'd forgotten where he was, who she was, as his fingers played in the thickness of her hair.

"Her hair was just like yours." His voice was low, husky with suppressed emotion. "Rich and thick..." The haunted look faded as the uncanny green glow in his eyes intensified. "But when I buried her, it wasn't so pretty anymore." He smiled tightly, as if satisfied by the look of terror that twisted Lindsey's features. "Don't push me, Lindsey. Twice you've entered into my domain and twice I've let you go free. Don't try a third time." With these words he turned and, moving with the silence and agility of a wild animal, he disappeared into the dark thickets.

When he was gone, Lindsey released a shuddery sigh. She willed her feet to move and carry her onto the path he'd designated as the way out of the swamp. Sure enough, within minutes she broke through the brush and saw Cindy's swimming pool, the blue water glittering with the last rays of day.

She went into the house and carefully locked the door, her thoughts a jumbled mass of chaos. She couldn't discount the fear he instilled in her. She couldn't suppress the shiver of apprehension that raced up her spine as she remembered the glow in his eyes as he spoke of burying the woman who'd ventured into the swamp before her.

And yet...she reached up and touched her hair, remembering the feel of his hand caressing it. When he'd touched her hair, there had been a wistfulness, a longing so intense in his eyes it had touched her deep within.

She pulled her hand from her hair, wondering if Jack the Ripper had caressed his victims' hair just before he'd killed them. The thought caused another shiver to dance up her spine.

She took the camera upstairs and set it on the antique dresser, pausing for a moment to look in the mirror, her reflection warped and slightly askew.

Her eyes were still widened, and she forced herself to relax. She was safe here, the house locked up tight as a drum. "No swamp boogers around here," she thought, remembering Charley Hawkins's expression. She was safe here in the house and she felt the last lingering tension seeping out of her.

She would be a fool to venture back into the swamp. He'd made it quite clear that he might not be kind enough to lead her out a third time.

She turned away from the mirror with a sigh, heading back downstairs to fix something to eat. As she placed a TV dinner into the microwave, she punched the buttons to make the machine hum, then leaned back against the cabinet, still deep in thought.

She could always plan a trip to the Okefenokee Swamp when Cindy Mae and Remy returned from Europe. She was probably less than a hundred miles from the famous swamp. She could finish out her photos there, without the worry of a demon-driven madman causing her physical harm. Yes, that was what she would do.

The microwave buzzed, signaling that her dinner was cooked and ready to eat. As she carried it to the kitchen table, she was struck by the silence of the house. It was a quiet much like the one that always signaled that Royce was near, although she knew there was no way possible he could be here in the safety of the house. The doors were securely locked, the windows tightly closed.

As she ate, she thought of that stillness that was so strange whenever Royce drew near. It was as if all the insects and noisemakers in the swamp felt his presence, cringed beneath the rage he suppressed, quieted and hid from the storm he carried within. What caused his anger? What demons drove him? Of course there was no answer, and speculation was useless.

CHAPTER FOUR

Lindsey moved from window to window, door to door, trying to discern how Royce had managed to get into the house. But she saw no signs of forced entry, no broken glass or unlocked window through which he could have entered. How on earth had he managed to get in?

She remembered that moment when she'd been fixing her dinner, when the silence of the house had suddenly pressed in on her. Had he been here then? Had that been the moment when he'd crept into the house?

He's just a man, she reminded herself. *He's made of flesh and blood. He's not some supernatural apparition, able to walk through walls or seep through cracks.*

Yet even the common sense spilling in her head couldn't stop the finger of fear that unfurled in her stomach and filled her with a sense of dread. Despite the fact that she was now certain every door and window in the house was securely locked, she felt vulnerable and utterly, completely alone.

She grabbed blankets and pillows off her bed and carried them downstairs to the sofa in the living room. There was no way she would sleep in the room where he'd been. At least in the living room, she was in the heart of the house with the telephone at arm's reach. Of course she had no idea who she'd call if she needed help. She had an idea that dialing 911 in a town the size of Baton Bay would prove ineffectual. She didn't allow herself to dwell on this fact.

She huddled beneath her blankets, sleep elusive as her mind whirled. Would he come back? Would he sneak up on her while she slept and fulfill the promise of his strong hands encircling her neck? Would he creep back in while she was vulnerable and let his insanity steal her life?

She jumped at each creak, every groan the house made as it settled for the night. One of the wooden shutters banging against the side of the house became his footsteps in the hall. The air conditioner kicking on became his breath in the room. The *ticktock* of the clock was his heartbeat.

Several times she got up off the sofa and went to the window to stare out into the impenetrable darkness, wondering if he was out there watching her...waiting for her.

She kept the lamp on the coffee table next to her turned on, the light a talisman against things that went bump in the night. She was afraid to sleep, fearing her dreams . . . afraid to stay awake, fearing reality.

It was a very long time before she finally drifted off into a sleep of sheer exhaustion.

She ran through the swamp, screaming as it came alive all around her. The cypress trees moved and swayed, blocking paths, forming impenetrable barriers to prevent her escape.

The moss beneath her feet grew dangerously slippery, further impeding her as she ran in panic. Flowers became animated, growing to enormous proportions, becoming malevolent creatures whose petals snapped open and closed with menacing strength.

The surface of the water all around her bubbled like a witch's caldron, hiding creatures who roiled and splashed in a frenzy. Vines grew, shooting out tendrils that coiled like snakes around her ankles. The Spanish moss cried overhead, an eery, keening noise as it reached down to claim her and hold her captive.

She tripped and fell, crying out as the swamp pulled her deeper into its bowels. As she fought to get away, she heard the sound of Royce's laughter echoing all around her....

She awoke slowly, kicking and whimpering as she fought through the layers of consciousness. Her struggles carried her over the edge of the sofa, and she landed on the floor with a thud, her legs tightly tangled in the twisted blankets.

She lay for a moment, orienting herself to her position on the floor and the bright sunshine that poured through the living room windows. She looked at her wristwatch and gasped in surprise. Ten o'clock. She lay on the floor for a moment, allowing her breathing to return to some semblance of normalcy.

"What a night," she muttered, untangling herself and standing up. At least no swamp boogers had made their way into the house.

She folded the blankets and scrubbed at her eyes. It had not been a restful sleep. She felt as if she'd fought for her very life all night long.

She headed for the bathroom, checking all the doors and windows before permitting herself the luxury of a soak in the tub.

In the brightness of morning, her terror of the night receded. Like a child clinging to hopes of dawn to chase away nightmares, Lindsey found exhausted relief in the break of day.

She lounged in the water, feeling taut muscles unkink, nerves relax. She'd made it through the night and felt the optimism of a prisoner on death row gaining a governor's pardon. She leaned her head back and expelled a grateful sigh.

She felt better after the bath, even managed to summon up a healthy dose of self-righteous anger as she looked at the broken camera lens. Damn him. What right did he have to break into the house and destroy her property?

Thank goodness she had several more camera lenses. Although less expensive, her spares would suffice.

It didn't matter how he had gotten into the house. She knew it was meant to be a final warning for her to stay away from the swamp.

It irked her, that this one man had appointed himself guardian of the swamp and refused to allow her in. She could have accepted it more easily if her job entailed something that could cause harm. But she was taking photographs. What possible harm could that cause?

"Madmen don't need reasons," she muttered to herself, dropping the lens into the trash. It was beyond repair. She added the curl of ribbon to the garbage as well, finding its silky length abhorrent.

She walked over to the window and gazed out at the area of contention. It didn't look scary or menacing this morning. With the brilliant sunshine dappling the place, surrounded by flowers who'd opened their blooms to the warmth of the sun, it looked beautiful and interesting, but certainly not forbidding.

"Damn that man," she cursed, turning away from the view that so compelled her.

After a light breakfast of tea and toast, the day stretched long and empty before her. She knew she could still take some great pictures without the telephoto lens, but she was reluctant to return to the swamp on the heels of Royce's threat. Who knew what the man was truly capable of? If the rumors were true, he was capable of plenty.

She spent the remainder of the morning dusting the furniture and vacuuming the carpet. She tried talking to Cindy's plants, but as she stood in front of them, the memory of the flora from her nightmare intruded, causing the words to bunch in her throat. The nightmare had been so vivid, so real despite the surreal aspects. There was no way she could sing some nonsensical song to plants that had tried to eat her in her dream.

As she passed the windows, she studiously kept her gaze away from the swamp, not wanting to think of the place or the man who'd haunted her sleep.

After lunch she sat down on the sofa and picked up a fashion magazine, needing something to occupy her mind. She thought about going swimming, but dismissed the idea. She didn't even want to be outside where *he* could spy on her from the secret hidey-holes of his precious swamp.

She was thumbing through the magazine when the phone rang.

"Lindsey, it's Verla."

Lindsey smiled at the sound of the woman's perky voice. "Hi, Verla."

"I was wondering if you'd like to meet me in town later this afternoon. Maybe catch a movie and get some dinner."

"That sounds great," Lindsey agreed immediately. Perhaps the time spent with the open, vivacious Verla would chase away the blues she'd experienced since awakening.

"Great! Why don't we meet in the same café where we talked yesterday…say around three. We can catch an early movie and a late supper."

"Okay, but not too late," Lindsey replied, wanting to be back in the house with the doors tightly locked before the darkness of night invaded the area.

After she hung up she realized how much she looked forward to it. She enjoyed Verla's company and found her an invaluable source of information concerning the area.

Besides, she could take her camera and get some shots of Baton Bay. She could do a pictorial on the quaint little town. And maybe... just maybe by talking to Verla she could gain some perspective on the madman of the swamp.

"You look just like a real photographer," Verla greeted her later that afternoon, gesturing to the camera hanging around Lindsey's neck.

"Or a tourist." Lindsey laughed and joined Verla at the table. Her spirits immediately perked up as she admired Verla's hot pink summer dress and matching earrings in the shape of flamingos. Her colorful dress could only be topped by the friendly sparkle in her bright blue eyes.

"You want a cup of coffee or something?" Verla asked. "We have about half an hour before the movie starts."

"That sounds great," Lindsey agreed. Verla gestured for the waitress, who immediately poured Lindsey a cup of the thick chicory brew.

"So, how are you getting along out there at Cindy Mae's place?" Verla asked when the waitress had departed.

"I'd be doing fine if it wasn't for the neighbors."

"Neighbors?" Verla's forehead wrinkled in perplexity. "You don't have any neighbors out there unless you count the swamp."

"Exactly. And it's one particular inhabitant of the swamp who's giving me trouble."

Verla's eyes flickered in comprehension, then narrowed. "You mean, Swamp Man... Royce Blanchard?" she asked in a whisper.

Lindsey nodded and went on to explain about her run-ins with Royce, beginning with the first time in the swamp and ending with the broken camera lens of the previous night.

"Whew." Verla whistled low beneath her breath. "If I were you, I think I'd be checking into a motel today. There's no way I'd stay out there in that isolated place by myself." She paused thoughtfully, then continued. "Are you sure all the windows and doors were locked?"

"Securely."

Verla shivered, causing her blond hair to bob around her head. "That's totally spooky. You wouldn't catch me staying one minute out there all by myself."

Lindsey smiled tightly. "He might be able to chase me out of the swamp, but I'll be damned if I'll let him force me out of Cindy Mae's house. I made a commitment to Cindy Mae and Remy."

"Ah, a woman of principles. I'll have that etched on your tombstone."

"Verla!" Lindsey protested. "That's a terrible thing to say."

"Yeah, well, messing around with the Swamp Man is a foolish thing to do," Verla returned. "You know the stories about him, and like I said the other day, where there's smoke, there's fire. Those rumors didn't just spring out of nowhere. There has to be a real reason for them.'' She shivered suddenly as if a blast of cold air had breathed on her spine.

Lindsey could think of no reasonable retort.

Later, sitting in the theater, surrounded by the scent of buttery popcorn and the soft murmurs of fellow moviegoers, Lindsey tried to focus her attention on the action taking place on the big screen before her. But her mind was filled with thoughts of Royce.

For her, the man held a curious blend of fascination and fear. It would have been easy to dismiss him as a madman if he'd come at her spouting gibberish or had gone swinging through the trees. But he hadn't. He was well-spoken, with a proud demeanor and arrogance that was attractive. He'd looked almost normal, if you didn't look too deep into those misty green eyes.

She thought of his eyes, the green hue that when focused on her had stirred something deep inside her. His skin had been that of a man who spent most of his time outside in the elements... bronzed, but without a hint of the leathery texture of many sun-worshippers.

She felt an invading warmth spread throughout her body as she thought of his hands circling her neck, caressing the length of her hair. She'd been so afraid. The memory of that terror even now made her breath catch in her chest. But what bothered her was that beneath that fear his touch had called up a latent sensuality. She had been able to easily imagine those same

strong hands caressing her body, evoking pleasurable
sensations.

Maybe I'm the one who is crazy, she thought with a
tight grimace. How else to explain that the first man
to attract her in months was a dangerous loony tune
who lived in a swamp?

Consciously dismissing him from her mind, she focused her attention on the movie screen before her,
where a car-chase scene held Verla enthralled.

"That wasn't bad," Verla commented as they
walked out of the theater some time later. She sighed
reluctantly and threw the last of her box of Junior
Mints away.

"It was all right," Lindsey agreed. "Although action films aren't my favorite."

"Let me guess...your favorite is a good romance." Verla laughed as Lindsey smiled. "I had a
feeling that beneath that camera hanging around your
neck beats the heart of a true romantic."

"Guilty as charged," Lindsey admitted with a small
grin. "What gave me away?" she asked as they began
the walk back toward the café.

"Several things. First of all, you'd have to have a
romantic, poetic heart to be a photographer. And
secondly, your fascination with the Swamp Man and
the stories that surround him." Verla grinned knowingly. "Only a true romantic would find him interesting. Normal people find him spooky."

"You have to admit, the stories about him are interesting," Lindsey protested. "Son of the devil, a

swamp witch for a mother...not everyone boasts such an impressive background.''

"You'd be surprised. This area is full of ghost stories and folklore,'' Verla explained. "There's the crying cypress trees, and then there's the ghost of Manor House..."

"Are these places in town?" Lindsey asked, her curiosity heightened. Verla nodded. "Can you show them to me?" Lindsey pressed.

Verla grinned and pushed open the door of the café. "First, we eat. Then I'll give you the official tour of Baton Bay's supernatural spooks."

Over dinner the two talked, offering little tidbits of past history to each other, strengthening their budding friendship. As they chatted, Lindsey discovered Verla had been divorced for four years and was actively seeking a Mr. Right Number Two.

"Good men are hard to find, true love even harder. I thought I had it with George, but the longer we were married the more positive I was I'd made a horrible mistake. The man was a slob, and if that wasn't bad enough, he was a selfish slob,'' Verla explained, smiling apologetically as she abandoned her fork and picked up her chicken with her fingers.

Lindsey did the same, finding the Cajun spiced poultry wonderful. As they ate, Lindsey shared her recent heartbreak, surprised to discover that the pain had eased somewhat over the past week. There had been a time when she'd not been able to imagine life without John. She was pleased to realize that now she had trouble imagining life *with* him.

"Well, I say good riddance," Verla said when Lindsey was finished with the details of John's infidelity. "You're better off without him. You've got too much going for you to put up with a creep like that." Her voice rang with indignity and the flamingo earrings danced wildly from her ears.

"My sentiments exactly," Lindsey agreed, feeling better than she had in weeks. She reached over and touched Verla's hand shyly. "Thanks, I needed to hear that."

Verla grinned irrepressibly. "You know what they say—when you fall off a horse, you're supposed to get right back on one." She gazed at Lindsey slyly. "As a matter of fact, I just happen to have a good friend. He's a wonderful guy with a good sense of humor. He's thirty-eight years old—"

"No way," Lindsey interrupted. "This is strictly a working vacation. I'm here to take pictures and house-sit for Cindy. I'm not interested in becoming involved with anyone right now."

"If you run across any eligible bachelors who like full-figured women, send them my way. I'm definitely interested in becoming involved."

"It's a deal," Lindsey agreed with a laugh.

After eating, they left the café and headed down the sidewalk toward the heart of the town. "This is small town Southern living at its best," Lindsey observed as she saw how many people were out enjoying the last hours of the day. It was a pleasant evening with a redolent breeze that caressed their faces as they entered the town park.

"Look." Verla pointed ahead where four cypress trees seemed to rise magically out of the concrete walkway. As Lindsey got closer, she noticed the sidewalk veered slightly, making way for the small pool of dark water that gave the trees their sustenance.

The trees, rising out of nowhere, with the glow of twilight providing a backdrop, looked strange and completely out of place.

"It's said that these trees once stood at the edge of the swamp, where a band of Indians made their home." Verla told the story as Lindsey clicked her camera shutter, capturing on film their unlikely resting place. "One day the Indians decided to move on. They packed up their things and moved inland. The trees mourned, missing the Indians who they'd come to love. They cried so long and so hard the ground around their roots grew soft, making it possible for them to uproot and go in search of the Indians. They finally found their Indian family here, and the trees have been here ever since."

"What a beautiful story," Lindsey exclaimed.

Verla led her around to the back of the trees and pointed to where the bark of one was misshapen. "Look, if you squint your eyes that looks like the face of a man crying. That's how the trees got the name of the crying cypress."

Lindsey took pictures, excited by the twilight's illumination playing on the trees, the strange pattern in the wood that, indeed, did look like the face of a tearful man. The story she mentally filed away to use as text with the photos.

From the trees Verla took her to Manor House, a two-story bed-and-breakfast where it was said that whenever there was a full moon, the ghost of a young girl walked the balcony of the second floor.

"Sounds like a good publicity story," Lindsey said dubiously.

"Possibly," Verla agreed. "At least with a story like that, the management is assured of a booked house once a month when there's a full moon."

Lindsey took half a dozen pictures. Whether the story of the ghost was true or not, the house had a certain interesting ambiance that she instinctively knew would transmit to photos.

They made their way back to the park, where they sat and rested on a semisecluded wooden bench backed by glorious mock orange bushes with their white flowers and fragrant scent of fruit.

"This is nice," Lindsey said, breathing deeply of the fragrant air and watching the people who were also out enjoying the mild evening. Couples milled around, lingering before the glorious flower beds. Mothers and fathers watched their children playing in the sandbox or swinging on the swing set. Young lovers held hands, gazing at nothing but each other.

"It's nice to see so many people out enjoying the evening," Lindsey observed. "In Washington, D.C., everyone always seems to be in a hurry."

Verla shrugged. "There's not much else to do in a town the size of Baton Bay. One movie theater, one café, a nightclub out on the edge of town... There aren't many diversions other than gossiping and enjoying the good weather.'' Verla stretched her plump legs out before her. "Besides, everyone had better enjoy this weather now. I heard this morning on the news that there's a storm working its way toward us."

"A hurricane?" Lindsey asked. She'd never been in one before and didn't know whether to be intrigued with the idea or scared.

"Nah, just a vicious low front."

"Still, it's nice right this minute." Lindsey sighed, completely relaxed. Her nightmares from the night before seemed distant. It was easy to dismiss her fears when surrounded by the laughter of children, the murmur of people visiting with each other, and with the scent of flowers filling her nose.

"What are you going to do when Remy and Cindy Mae get home?" Verla asked.

"I'm really not sure. If my pictures sell, I might continue to travel and put together some kind of a travelogue. I've got a little savings put away and really don't have to make any decision for a month or two." Lindsey leaned her head back and closed her eyes. "I can always get another job as a secretary."

"Yuck, being a photographer sounds much more exciting," Verla exclaimed.

Lindsey nodded, feeling almost drowsy with relaxation. "Ouch!" she yelped suddenly as she felt a sudden vicious tug on her hair. She slapped her hand on the injured spot and turned around.

"What's the matter?" Verla asked in surprise.

"Somebody pulled my hair," Lindsey exclaimed, peering through the thick bush behind her, trying to see if somebody hid there.

Verla also turned around. "I don't see anyone." She got up and circled the bushes behind the bench, then sat back down beside Lindsey. "Nobody there." She frowned. "Why would anyone want to pull your hair? Are you sure it wasn't a bug bite of some kind? We've got mosquitoes out here the size of washtubs."

"I don't know, it didn't feel like a bite." Lindsey rubbed the tender spot with her fingers.

"Here, let me see." Verla moved around behind Lindsey and gently parted her hair. "Wow, it does look like somebody yanked out a hunk of your hair. Your scalp is all red and raw."

Once again they both looked around, intently studying the people sharing the park with them. "Maybe it was kids," Verla finally offered. "You know, a dare of some kind or another."

"Yeah, probably," Lindsey agreed, although she found the whole thing disturbing. The contented mood of moments before was shattered. Besides, the early evening light was waning. "I guess I'll head on home," she said, standing up, her fingertips lingering on the back of her scalp.

It suddenly seemed vital that she get home before the darkness of night. She quickened her pace down the sidewalk to where her car was parked.

"Are you sure you're all right?" Verla asked, eyeing her worriedly as she tried to keep up with Lindsey's fast pace.

"I'm fine. I'm sure you're probably right, it was just some childish prank." She gave Verla a reassuring smile. "Besides, I'm not going to let one little sneaky prankster ruin what's been a very enjoyable day."

"I enjoyed it, too," Verla replied, pausing by the car as Lindsey dug in her purse for her keys. "We'll have to do it again real soon."

"I'm game for everything except another hair-jerking," Lindsey said. She got into her car and waved goodbye to Verla. "Call me," she yelled to her new friend as she took off.

Once on the road heading back to Cindy's, her hand again reached for the back of her head, probing the area with her fingertips. Weird…the whole thing was strange. If it had been nothing but a kid's prank, then Lindsey hoped it was one kid whose backside would be warmed by a firm parental hand.

Still, it had been a pleasant day. She'd enjoyed Verla's company and was excited to get the pictures of the town developed. She had a feeling she'd snapped some really good pictures.

She touched the back of her head once again, unable to shake a horrible sense of foreboding. She gazed up into the sky, noting the fingers of night's darkness slowly reaching out to capture the last of dusk. She stepped down on the gas pedal, needing to outrace them, wanting to be in the house before night grabbed the light in its hands.

By the time she pulled up in front of the house, the last rays of daylight were slowly disappearing behind the swamp, giving the whole area a coppery glow.

She lingered by the car, more at ease now that she stood in front of the house. Her attention was captured by the marshland. How was it that such an area could evoke such ambiguous emotions? She felt both attracted and repelled. She was drawn to it and wanted to run from it at the same time. It was a strange feeling, this magnetic pull mingling with a sense of dread.

Her eyes narrowed as she thought she saw movement at the edge of the thicket. Was he standing there, watching her? In her state of mind it was easy to imagine him in the shape of a tree, a shadow of the night. And never far from her thoughts was the fact that he'd managed to get into the house once. Could he do it again? Disgusted with her own fanciful imagination, she turned and walked toward the front door.

If she had to guess, she thought the way he'd probably gotten in to break her camera lens was through a door she'd inadvertently left unlocked. There was nothing spooky or supernatural about it. She'd been careless, he'd come in, then locked the door as he left. She smiled approval at her rational explanation.

As she reached the top step of the veranda, the smile faded as her gaze focused on something lying just outside the front door. Moving closer, she frowned in confusion. A doll. What on earth was a child's doll doing lying at her front door?

As she knelt down to get a better look, an icy chill pierced through her and fear convulsed her insides. It was not some child's toy as she'd first thought. It was not just any doll, but a voodoo doll.

Made of wax, obviously female, it was crudely fashioned without features. A twig had fallen across the doll's head. Lindsey reached out and removed the twig. She gasped, and stuffed the knuckles of one hand into her mouth while the other hand automatically went to the back of her head. Hair. Attached to the doll's head were strands of what looked to be her own curly dark hair. And around the neck was a bright yellow ribbon.

With trembling hands, she gingerly picked up the doll, then stumbled to her feet. She looked around, her gaze immediately going to the swamp. Was he there, watching her? Could he feel her fear? Hadn't the broken camera lens been enough? Why this? She rubbed the back of her head again. How had he managed it?

She fumbled with the door lock, her hands trembling, afraid that at any moment she was going to be sick.

Royce stood at the edge of the swamp long after she'd disappeared into the house. His body radiated tension, the effects of tightly reined emotion.

He could still remember the feel of her slender neck beneath the power of his hands. So vulnerable, so weak... He trembled at the memory.

It was getting more and more difficult for him to master his disturbed thoughts, fight the demons that threatened to suffocate his sanity.

She had to leave... had to escape before he lost the last vestige of control, before the same old madness overtook him.

CHAPTER FIVE

Lindsey sat on the sofa, staring mutely at the doll lying on the coffee table. "I don't believe in voodoo. I don't believe in voodoo." She repeated the words like a litany against evil.

She knew little about voodoo and curses. It was something she'd seen in movies, read a little bit about in books. But she had no real knowledge of the workings of it. She'd always thought that it wouldn't work unless the cursed person truly believed.

So why did she now have a pounding headache in the exact same spot where the twig had been lying across the doll's head?

Power of suggestion, she told herself firmly. Power of suggestion and nerves, that was what made her head ache. At least there were no pins or needles stuck in the wax effigy, she thought, touching the ribbon with one finger.

It's not meant to harm me, just to frighten me. As this thought came to mind, she recognized the truth of it. Had somebody meant to do her harm, they would have carried it through and placed needles in vital places. They would have kept the doll instead of leaving it for her to find.

Foolishness...that was all it was. Foolishness intended to frighten her. Straightening her shoulders and taking a deep breath, she picked up the offending object and carried it into the kitchen. She tromped on the lever of the trash can, popping the top open. She held the doll over the dark plastic liner, willing her fingers to open and release it, discard it like the garbage it was. But her fingers refused to cooperate. There was a small part of her that was afraid to just throw it away.

She allowed the garbage pail lid to slam closed. "Now what?" she muttered. *How do I go about getting rid of a voodoo doll?* It was definitely a question she never dreamed she'd ever have to contemplate.

Burn it. The words pounded in her head, intensifying the headache that grew more pronounced with each passing minute.

In all the horror movies she'd ever seen, wasn't it usually fire that neutralized evil? Or did fire sustain evil? She refused to let this last thought linger.

Holding the doll in one hand, with the other she dug through several kitchen drawers, finally finding a cache of matchbooks. Grabbing one, she carried the wax figure back into the living room and set it in the ornate crystal ashtray that was in the center of the coffee table.

She stared at the doll for a long moment, her hands trembling as she pulled a match from the book. She struck the match, the scent of sulfur instantly assaulting her senses. She guided the burning end toward the offending object. Before it touched the figure, she gasped and shook the flame out.

She couldn't do it. She just couldn't burn it. Even thinking about it made her internal body temperature climb twenty degrees. She'd read somewhere about spontaneous combustion, the strange phenomenon that made people suddenly burst into flames. Had there ever been a scientific study to see if these people had burned voodoo dolls of themselves?

Knowing she was being silly, she leaned back on the sofa and rubbed her temple where the headache speared her. She would place the doll in the china cabinet where no harm would befall it. It was silly, it was crazy, but she was afraid to destroy it in any way.

One thing was certain. She would not venture back into the swamp. Royce had been responsible for her broken camera lens, he'd been responsible for the wax effigy—he'd won. She wasn't about to go back into his domain and tempt the Fates. If the man was truly insane, as everyone seemed to think he was, then she wasn't about to discover how far he would go to keep her out. This was more than far enough.

For the next three days, Lindsey kept herself busy taking photos of interesting spots near the town of Baton Bay, discovering other places of photogenic beauty to indulge her passion.

Yet, no matter how far she drove during the day to take pictures, no matter how involved she got in her work, she always planned it so she would return to the house long before dark.

Sleep didn't come until she'd checked and re-checked each and every window and door in the house. She found herself walking by the china cabinet several times a day, just to check and make certain the doll was still there, still unharmed.

She'd taken up permanent residency on the sofa in the living room, not wanting to be upstairs in a bedroom should anything happen.

During the days, she managed to forget all about the presence of the swamp, the aura of suppressed violence and mystery that surrounded Royce.

It was only at night as she lay in her bed that the swamp called to her. It sang its song of whispered wind and frog croaks, strange bird cries and insect chatter. Each night it pulled her up the stairs and through the French doors to the balcony, where she'd sit long into the night, staring at the eerie silhouette of cypress trees and moonlit terrain.

Each night she wondered if he was there, watching her as she watched the swamp. She could almost visualize him standing at the edge of the brush, his bronzed torso blending in with the bark of the trees, his unusual green gaze able to see through the darkness of the night with the accuracy of a wild animal.

She knew she was being fanciful, attributing to him supernatural powers, but twice as she sat on the balcony, the noise from the swamp halted, leaving an empty silence that caused goose bumps to stir on her arms. And she knew he was near...very near. Both times this had happened, she'd immediately returned to the house, going downstairs to snuggle under the blankets, longing for the comfort of dreamless sleep to wipe away the disturbing thoughts of Royce.

She awoke on the fourth morning, knowing instinctively the storms Verla had been predicting for the past three days were imminent. The sun streamed into the bedroom with an intense glare, forecasting an unusually hot day.

As she stepped out the back door with a cup of coffee, the humidity nearly knocked her over, immediately making it difficult to breathe and coating her skin in a light perspiration. Despite the fact that the sky was a brilliant blue, Lindsey knew that the heat and oppressive humidity were telling signs that the blue skies wouldn't be here for long. There was an electricity, an anticipation in the air, foretelling the coming of a storm.

As she sipped her coffee, her gaze automatically swept to the bog. The early morning light painted it in tones of yellows and golds, and she resented the man who'd forced her to choose to stay away from it.

She finished her coffee and went back inside, deciding she would just spend the day puttering around the house.

She felt lethargic and decided a day of just being lazy would be good for her. With this thought in mind, she found a book that looked interesting and curled up on the sofa.

It was nearly two o'clock when she surfaced out of the fictitious world, closed the romance novel and sighed with contentment. Boy meets girl, they fall in love and live happily ever after. That was the way it was supposed to work, she thought. It had worked that way for Cindy and Remy and dozens of Lindsey's other friends. So why hadn't it been like that for her?

When she'd met John, she'd been ready to make a lifetime commitment. She'd thought he felt the same. "You're a rotten judge of character," she muttered, pulling herself up off the sofa and heading into the kitchen for a late lunch.

She fixed herself a peanut butter and jelly sandwich and stood once again at the back door, her gaze shooting up to the sky where dark clouds now gathered beyond the swamp.

The clouds were black, hanging low enough that they seemed to grow out of the tops of the trees. The dark mass moved, shaping and reshaping, seeming to possess a malevolent life-force and energy.

Lindsey moved away from the door, oddly disturbed by nature's show of seething turbulence. She finished her sandwich, noting that the sunlight had disappeared, swallowed up by the fast-approaching storm clouds.

Turning on the transistor radio that sat on the kitchen cabinet, she wheeled the tuning dial, trying to pick up a weather report amid the static.

"...storm is tracking north and packing seventy-five to one hundred mile-per-hour winds. Batten down the hatches, folks, it's going to be a long night."

Terrific, a long night . . . as if having a crazy man as your nearest neighbor didn't make the nights long enough, she thought ruefully. She turned off the radio and headed upstairs where she went from room to room, closing and locking the wooden shutters that would protect the windows from breakage if necessary. Hopefully, the brunt of the storm would move on up the coast or out to the ocean where it could expend its fury harmlessly.

Once all the shutters were tightly closed, she turned on several lights to chase away the invading gloom. She'd never particularly minded storms in the past, but there was something about this house and its location that made the thought of a storm daunting.

She'd just settled back on the sofa when the phone rang. "Cindy!" she exclaimed in surprise, hearing the faint, tinny voice of her friend.

"Lindsey, how's everything there?"

"Fine, where are you?"

"Gay Paree. Wait until you see the two dresses Remy bought for me, you'll die! They're originals! How are my plants? Are you singing to them every day?"

"Everything is fine, and I can't wait to see your dresses," Lindsey laughed, delighted at the sound of Cindy's familiar, breathless voice. "Oh, while I have you on the line, I wanted to ask you about Royce Blanchard." Lindsey winced as the line suddenly filled with crackling static. "Cindy? Are you there?" she yelled into the receiver.

"...here...terrible connection," Cindy answered. "Royce is..." Again the line filled with fuzz.

"Cindy, I can't hear you.... What did you say about Royce?" Lindsey grabbed the phone more tightly to her ear.

"I said he's . . ." More static filled the line, forcing Lindsey to hold the receiver away from her ear. When she returned it to her ear, the connection was dead. She clicked the button several times, hoping for a miraculous reconnection, but the line remained dead.

She replaced the receiver slowly, thoughtfully, shivering as a sudden thought speared through her. The connection had been fine, as clear as a bell, until she'd mentioned *his* name.

Honestly, Lindsey, she admonished herself. She was letting the heebie-jeebies steal away her common sense. It had been an overseas connection in the middle of an approaching storm. Little wonder why it had been bad. It was only coincidence that had made the phone disconnect just as Cindy was telling her something about Royce.

She moved back over to the back door, staring up once again at the approaching storm. The dark clouds now pretty much consumed the sky. The sun made a valiant effort, piercing through in several places, sending skinny shafts of light down to the earth. The effort was beautiful, a perfect display of the opposing forces of light and dark. Light and dark, good and evil . . . the conflict as old as time itself.

She left the back door, racing up the stairs for her camera. She wanted to capture the contrast on film, knowing she could get some great pictures of the storm before it broke its restraints.

The air was still hot, heavy with humidity as she ventured out to the backyard, but the wind had picked up, sending out chill gusts as a forewarning of the coming tempest.

The shafts of sunlight that had been there only moments before were gone, swallowed up by the bubbling, black clouds that now spewed lightning and rumbled in displeasure.

Lindsey snapped the shutter as fast as she could, knowing she was getting some terrific shots as she focused on the dark swamp. Lightning exploded, illuminating the area, turning the Spanish moss into silver shrouds, the trees to otherworldly silhouettes.

Finally, exhausting her roll of film, she sat down on one of the chaise longues near the pool, content just to be a spectator to nature's display of temperament. The lightning was still in the distance, the thunder an echo several seconds later. When the storm moved closer and the lightning got dangerously near, she would go inside. In the meantime, she watched the skies, smelling the tempest as it gathered strength.

She was just about to go in when she heard a dog yipping. She looked around, surprised to see a collie sitting at the edge of the yard. The dog barked several times, then advanced warily toward her.

"Hey, boy, where did you come from?" Lindsey set her camera down on the ground next to her chair and extended her hand out to the dog. He approached slowly, his nose sniffing suspiciously at her hand. Apparently he found her a friend, for he licked her hand and sat down on the ground beside her.

"Hey, fellow, where do you belong?" It was obvious the dog wasn't a stray. His coat was too clean and he looked too well fed. She felt around his neck for a collar, but there was none. "Are you lost or did you run away?" she asked, smiling as he barked an answer to her question. He barked again, the bark turning into a whine as thunder rumbled overhead and a gust of wind whipped against them.

"It's okay, boy. It's just a storm," she said, laughing as he nuzzled her neck with his cold nose. "You really are a sweetie," she murmured, stroking down his back, then laughing again as he rolled over to allow her access to his belly. He rolled back over and stood up, tense as thunder once again roared around them.

"Come on, boy. You can come in with me for the night." Lindsey patted the dog's neck and looked up at the sky. "This is going to be a heck of a night. Not even a dog should be out." She hoped the mutt was house-trained, and if not, she hoped Cindy Mae's carpet was stain-resistant. But she couldn't let the storm break and leave the poor dog outside.

She took a couple of steps and called for the dog to follow her. He ran toward her, then veered off, barking like they were playing a game. "Come on," Lindsey urged him, laughing as he darted all around her. He circled her several times, his tongue hanging out, making her laugh again at his silly antics. Her laughter faded as a bolt of lightning danced across the sky, immediately followed by a clap of thunder that made a scream jump into her throat.

The dog took off, running toward the swamp, obviously terrified. "Hey, come back here," Lindsey yelled after him. She muttered a curse as she heard the heartrending whines of the frightened dog. She could just barely see him in the underbrush, cowering with fear. Casting a quick look upward, knowing the storm could unleash its full fury at any moment, Lindsey quickly ran toward where the dog hid.

"Come on, boy, I'll cook you a big steak when we get inside," she said, cursing again as he took off running farther into the swamp. She followed after him, shouting encouragements and enticements to the frightened animal, but he ignored her, whining loudly as he ran.

So intent was she on getting the dog to safety, she didn't realize she'd ventured farther in than she ever had before. And more frightening than anything was that the storm had breathed new life into the swamp. The wind blew with a vengeance, making the trees creak and groan. The bushes swelled and swayed as if alive, rustling as if full of animals.

As the first raindrops splashed her face, she realized she needed to go back. She no longer saw the dog. She no longer heard his barks and whines. She couldn't hear anything except the thunder and the moaning shriek of the wind. *You're on your own, dog,* she thought, turning around to retrace her steps.

Panic welled up in her throat as she realized she didn't know how to retrace her steps. She'd been so busy running after the dog she hadn't paid attention

to direction. And to make matters worse, the storm
broke overhead.

Like a wild animal suddenly released from a re-
strictive cage, the storm was eager to vent its anger,
anxious to destroy. Lindsey's ears filled with a loud
roar as she ran through the swamp, trying desperately
to find her way out of the thicket. The rain fell in earnest, pelting her face and shoulders painfully. She
lowered her head, crying out as the brush lashed at
her. The panic in her throat spread throughout her
body, forcing her breath to escape in gasps, her legs to
move like wooden sticks.

She paused suddenly, cocking her head to one side
as a new sound penetrated through the roar. A baby
crying? She closed her eyes, concentrating on filter-
ing out all other sounds. Yes... yes, it was there, carrying on the wind... a baby's cry. What on earth was
a child doing out here in the swamp in the middle of a
storm?

The panic she'd been experiencing suddenly transformed to terror...sheer terror as she remembered the
stories of Royce and the murdered baby. What was it
Verla had said? Something about being able to hear
the cries of the murdered baby riding on the wind?

It's crazy... dead babies don't cry, Lindsey told
herself rationally. So...what was she hearing? Afraid
of the answer, Lindsey ran, grunting and screaming as
the swamp seethed around her, lashing out at her with
all the fury of the devil's ire. She stumbled to one
knee, pulled down by the moss which had become a
sucking muck. She pulled herself up and ran on,

fighting both the ferocity of the storm and the elements of the swamp.

The rain slashed at her, pelting her with harsh drops that stung her skin. The wind ripped at her, forcing her to fight to stand upright. She screamed as a tree tumbled over, blocking her path. She turned and ran blindly in another direction.

The world had turned upside down, tossed helter-skelter by Mother Nature's foul mood. Lindsey felt as if she were caught in a vortex of energy, lost in a place where there was no escape. She was in her nightmare, and the swamp worked to capture her forever. But she couldn't wake up and escape from this dream.

And the crying... the insistent keening of the baby... she stopped running, still hearing the haunting cries. She gasped and slammed her palms against her ears, wondering if she were losing her mind.

"Lindsey."

She spun around at the deep voice that thundered her name loud enough to shake the moss beneath her feet. She turned to see Royce, his eyes blazing with the same intensity as the storm that surrounded them. He was like an image from a nightmare, his long hair rain-slicked, his eyes glowing with a fiery heat.

He advanced toward her and she stepped back... terrified of him. He seemed to be as much a part of the storm as the wind and the thunder. His eyes reflected the madness that surrounded them.

She took another step backward, hearing a loud crackling overhead. She looked up just in time to see a heavy tree limb split from the trunk and come crashing down. She didn't have time to step aside. She didn't even have time to release the scream that was trapped in her throat. There was a moment of intense pain in her head, then nothing.

Royce walked to where Lindsey lay crumpled on the ground, her head bleeding from the glancing blow it had received. He stared down at her, his eyes narrowed as he considered options. He could leave her here and she would probably die. The storm had only just begun and was still far from its zenith. She would probably die from exposure or any other number of natural causes.

With a heavy sigh he picked her up and threw her over his shoulder. Despite the storm he moved swiftly toward his home, deep in the center of the swamp. Her weight across his shoulders didn't slow him down.

He climbed the stairs to his cabin, kicking open the door, then slamming it closed behind him. He deposited her on the small cot against one wall, then lit the kerosene lantern that sat in the center of the wooden table. He didn't even look at her as he took off his shoes and shrugged out of his wet jeans. He pulled on a dry pair, listening to the storm raging outside.

He liked storms, found that they reflected the turmoil he carried in his soul. The wind growled and shrieked like a creature from hell. The thunder bellowed in angry retort. Royce smiled, finding comfort in nature's rage.

Clad in dry clothes, he looked across the room to where she lay. Plastered to her scalp, her hair was soaked and muddied. The streak of blood on her forehead was a startling contrast to the paleness of her face. Her T-shirt and jeans were wet, clinging to her slender frame with taunting results.

Damn her...he'd told her time and again to stay out of here, stay away from him. His eyes narrowed as he stared at her. She hadn't listened. She hadn't heeded his warnings. So now, she had to face the consequences.

Lindsey swam through layers of fog to reach consciousness. It came in varying degrees, confusing her as her mind whirled. Her head hurt. That was her first conscious thought. It was a piercing pain that made thoughts of movement impossible, made coherent thought unreachable.

She was warm and dry, and for some reason this knowledge brought more confusion. It was raining. She could hear the relentless drum of water splattering on the roof.

Her thoughts were jumbled like the scattered pieces of a jigsaw puzzle. She kept her eyes closed, feeling the need to make sense of her thoughts before allowing the additional input of vision.

Fleeting images danced in her brain...running...out of breath...thunder overhead...plants reaching out, grabbing her...trees crashing down...hands of heat.

She caught and focused on the last confusing image. Vague memories fluttered through her brain. Hot hands slowly unbuttoning her blouse, moving it off her shoulders, leaving imprints of fire where they contacted her flesh. Strong hands tugging off her jeans...a muttered curse hissed against her neck. These images somehow seemed more real than the previous ones. Were they part of a disturbing dream? She could feel the sensation of those burning hands on her still. And something else...eyes...eyes the color of moss. Royce's eyes.

She sucked in her breath as memories came tumbling back, the pieces of the jigsaw puzzle locked into place. She remembered...the dog...the ferocity of the storm...Royce...the falling tree limb.

She opened her eyes to see a rough-hewn woodbeamed ceiling. She frowned again in confusion. Her head suddenly pounded with a new nauseating intensity as she realized where she was. Royce's cabin. She knew it with a certainty in her soul. Where else could she be? At the same time, she became aware of the fact that beneath the blanket that rested on top of her she wore only her panties and bra.

Those strangely erotic images whispered through her mind again. Had he undressed her? Had it been his hands that she'd felt on her body? His breath whispered against the base of her neck? Fear crept up her throat. My God, what was she doing here? She had to get out.

She turned her head toward the kerosene lantern that glowed from the table in the center of the room. Although the light illuminated brightly the area surrounding the table, it cast deep shadows into the corners of the room.

It was in one darkened corner that she saw him sitting, his gaze intently focused on her.

"You were warned," he said, his voice ominously soft.

Lindsey worked her mouth but could get no sound to escape from her terror-squeezed throat. With a small sigh, she allowed herself to be dragged back into the blankness of unconsciousness.

CHAPTER SIX

Lindsey opened her eyes, consciousness coming immediately this time. She had no idea how much time had lapsed since she'd allowed herself to fall back into the blackness of oblivion. It might have been minutes. It could have been hours.

The storm still raged outside, like a frenzied animal flinging itself against the cabin walls in a fit of self-destruction. She could hear the wind shrieking like an enraged phantom, trees scraping sharp talons against the cabin's exterior.

Even without turning her head to look, she knew Royce was still there in the darkened corner. She could feel his presence, sense the darkness of his soul. It made her heart pound painfully in her chest. She squeezed her eyes tightly closed, wishing it was possible to will herself to another place, another time.

She moved her head slightly, aware of a new sound. It was a rhythmic scraping noise that set her teeth on edge and filled her with an inexplicable sense of dread.

She moved her head a little more and cracked her eyes open slightly, trying to discern the source of the strange noise.

He'd moved his chair up closer to the table, the kerosene lantern's glow finding and emphasizing the harsh lines of his face. He held a large knife in his hand, and the sound she heard was him scraping the knife down the length of a piece of wood.

She watched for a moment in dreadful fascination, mesmerized as the knife caught and reflected the lantern's glow.

She squeezed her eyes tightly closed again. She'd never felt so helpless, so frightened in her life. She had a vivid mental picture of the way his face had looked when he'd yelled at her before the limb had knocked her unconscious. Rage . . . it had been there, twisting his features into a mask of horror.

She was now afraid to open her eyes, afraid to make a sound, scared she would inadvertently do something that would invoke that mindless anger. And the last thing she wanted to do was make him mad when he had a weapon in his hand.

Her head ached, and she stifled the impulse to reach up and explore her wound. Her heart fluttered painfully in her chest as she thought of the strange doll she'd so carefully placed in Cindy Mae's china cabinet to keep it from harm. She bit down on her bottom lip to capture a burst of hysterical laughter that threatened to escape. She'd been so careful. She hadn't realized the damned doll was already cursed.

Had he sat in that very chair, carefully crafting the wax doll in her image? Had he mumbled some strange, secret dark words, summoning demons from another world? Then had he meticulously placed the twig just so, ensuring that she would be hit in the head by the falling tree limb?

Her hand inched up beneath the blankets, moving to touch the injured area of her head. It felt wet, sticky, and she knew it was blood. An uncontainable moan escaped her lips.

The scraping noise stopped abruptly, replaced by a thick silence. Outside the storm raged, and inside a storm of a different kind seemed to be brewing as the silence grew.

Lindsey knew he was looking at her. She could feel the heat of his gaze on her skin, lingering on her face, her bare shoulders. She fought her desire to yank the blanket up over her head, burrow so deeply into the mattress he'd never find her again. Instead she feigned unconsciousness, willing her breaths to come slowly, regularly despite her agitation.

"You're a stupid fool, Lindsey Witherspoon." His voice was deep and rich, filling up the entire area of the small cabin.

She didn't move, didn't flinch, feeling more safe in pretending unconsciousness. He laughed, a low chuckle that sent shivers skittering up and down her spine.

"You think that if you close your eyes and can't see me, it makes you invisible to my sight?" The scraping sound began again. "You were warned again and again to stay away from here. What on earth possessed you to venture back into the swamp in the middle of a storm?"

"A dog." Lindsey opened her eyes and looked at him fully for the first time. She saw a flicker of surprise cross his features.

"A dog?" he repeated dubiously.

Lindsey moaned, easing herself up to a sitting position, clutching the blanket to her chest as if it was a shield of armor. "A collie, to be more precise." She winced slightly, her head throbbing painfully. "He was afraid of the storm and I tried to get him into the house until it passed. He ran into the swamp and I ran after him."

With an explosive curse, he drove the tip of the knife deep into the tabletop. His eyes glittered phosphorescently, like mysterious rocks from an alien planet. "But you were told not to come back here."

"I didn't mean to," Lindsey gasped, fixated on the knife, which gleamed in the lantern light. "I was running after the dog, not paying any attention.... Then I couldn't find the dog and I heard... I heard a baby crying..." She shivered as she remembered the plaintive cry of the child. She looked at him again, searching his face. "I heard a baby crying," she repeated.

"Haven't you heard the stories? They're the cries of my murdered son." His eyes glittered strangely, and Lindsey felt as if her heart would explode in her chest.

"Dead babies don't cry," she whispered.

"Mine does." He pulled the knife out of the table and stood up. For a moment his gaze, black and empty, held hers. "Mine does," he repeated, then he opened the cabin door and disappeared out into the darkness of the storm.

Lindsey expelled a shuddery sigh. She had to get out of here. She had to leave before he came back, before his madness made him lose control and do something to harm her.

The first thing she had to do was find her clothes. She didn't even want to consider the fact that it had been Royce who had removed them from her body.

She pulled herself out of the bed, staggering as her head reeled with dizziness. She clutched the quilt around her like a sarong, closing her eyes for a moment as her knees buckled weakly. She reached up and touched her wound, swallowing hard against a choking nausea.

She took a deep breath, then opened her eyes again, feeling the wave of nausea slowly abating. Cautiously she took a step, expelling a grateful sigh as her legs worked to carry her over to the table. She leaned heavily on it and looked around curiously.

The cabin surprised her. The way Verla Sue had talked, she'd assumed Royce's living quarters were a dirty, run-down shanty, but the cabin was well-constructed with rich wood furnishings that gleamed with cleanliness. There was a gas stove and a small refrigerator, although she saw no electrical outlets or light switches. A wood-burning stove stood ready for the winter, a pile of split logs on the floor next to it. Strange-looking plants hung overhead from the rafters and again Lindsey shivered, wondering if he used the strange vegetation in ancient voodoo ceremonies.

She turned around, spying two doorways. Maybe her clothes were in one of those rooms. She made her way to the first door and opened it, surprised to see a modern bathroom complete with shower stall. The room was apparently an addition to the original structure, small but adequate. Lindsey moved in front of the wood-framed mirror that hung above the sink, gasping as she viewed her reflection.

She looked horrible. Her hair was tangled and wild around her shoulders. Her face was ghostly pale, her eyes dark with shadows beneath, but it was the angry blood-streaked welt across her forehead that made her stomach convulse sickly.

She turned on the water faucet, grimacing as the sink began to fill with faintly discolored liquid. Scooping the tepid water in her hands, she dabbed at the wound, rinsing off the dried blood, then taking a closer look. It didn't look quite as bad with the blood washed off, although she suspected she'd suffered a mild concussion. She clung for a moment to the sink, taking deep gulps of air, hoping the intake of oxygen would make her feel stronger.

She left the bathroom and opened the second door, finding a bedroom. The bed was neatly made, with a faded patchwork quilt. A kerosene lantern flickered from the wooden nightstand. It didn't look like the room of a madman. But then, Lindsey wasn't sure exactly what the bedroom of a lunatic was supposed to look like. All she knew was that her clothes were no place to be seen.

She froze in place as above the storm she heard the crying of a child. It was faint and distant, but distinctly a baby's cry. It was the same sound she'd heard just before Royce had come upon her in the swamp.

She made her way to the window next to the bed and pushed it open. The storm crawled in—rain pelted her face and wind whipped her hair. She swiped her eyes with the back of her hand, cocking her head to one side, and listened intently.

Yes...there it was...the cries of a child. "It's real," she said aloud. It was as real as the rain wetting her face, the wind that played in her hair. She cupped her hands on the sides of her eyes, trying to peer out, see where the sound emanated from, but the night was too dark, the storm too fierce. She could see nothing.

The cries swirled over her, through her, tugging insistently at her heart. The child sounded so unhappy. Pick him up, she wanted to scream. Somebody pick him up. Love him . . . soothe him . . . do something to make him stop crying.

She whirled around as the door to the cabin opened, then slammed shut. Terror, stark and white, whipped through her as Royce appeared at the bedroom door, dripping with rain, his face rigid with savage anger. He was a warrior come to pillage and rape, a warlock about to suck out her soul.

She backed against the wall, trying to disappear as he moved across the room and slammed shut the window. "What in the hell are you doing in here?" he asked, his voice harsh and demanding.

"I...I was looking for my clothes," she gasped, the unsanded wood of the wall scraping painfully into her back as she pressed into it in an attempt to melt away. "I heard it again...the baby...it's crying right now."

It suddenly seemed vital to her that he hear, that he acknowledge what she heard. She hurried back over to the window and pushed it open once again. "Listen . . ." she exclaimed, urging him closer to the window, where the cries were still audible above the sound of nature's violence.

He strode over next to her, bringing with him the scent of the storm and a tension that raised the hairs on Lindsey's arms. "Don't you hear it?" she asked, trying to ignore the oppressive closeness of him standing next to her. She stared at him, needing desperately for him to validate what she heard.

"There's nothing to hear," he contradicted, once again slamming the window shut.

"But there is. . . ."

"I said there's nothing. It's your imagination," he exploded, the fire in his eyes sparking in anger.

Lindsey stared at him for a long moment, then sagged in despair. Was she losing her mind? Were the cries only a figment of her imagination? Oh God, was lunacy contagious?

Her head pounded with a new intensity and a wave of nausea swept over her once again, making her stumble backward.

She gasped as he grabbed her and with one swift movement picked her up in his arms. His body heat seared through the quilt she had wrapped around her, heating her with a warmth that felt feverish. She wanted to fight against him, but it was as if the strength of him sucked the life out of her.

"No," she managed to utter, trying to hold her body stiff, unyielding to his arms. But it took too much effort, and she was suddenly overwhelmingly tired. She relaxed, giving in to the inevitable. She had no physical defenses against him. She had surpassed fear and moved into the realm of weary resignation.

He carried her through the bedroom door and lay her on the cot in the main room. "Lie down and go to sleep." He stood above her like a towering tree, his eyes flaming into hers.

"Please... just give me my clothes and let me go home," Lindsey replied, struggling weakly to get off the bed.

He placed his hands on her shoulders, his touch burning her as he pushed her back onto the mattress. "Go to sleep, Lindsey. There's no escape for you tonight."

No escape tonight. How bleak, how final those words sounded to her. She dutifully closed her eyes, too weary to protest, too frightened to resist doing as he told her. Her mind was overstimulated, too many images flitting through it in rapid succession. The storm, the knife with its wicked gleaming edge, his eyes wild and frightening... it was all too much.

She heard him move back over to the table, and the scraping noise began again. Rhythmically, the noise filled the room.

Lindsey realized that as long as the noise remained steady, it meant he was preoccupied with carving the wood. It was only when the sound stopped that she needed to be afraid.

* * *

Royce watched her as the knife worked back and forth, peeling off the layer of bark from the piece of cypress.

He knew the exact moment she fell asleep. Her chest rose and fell slowly and regularly, and her mouth fell slightly open. She moaned several times, as if fighting off nightmarish images. He waited a few more minutes to make certain she was deeply, soundly asleep. He then put his carving away and went into his bedroom.

He took off all his clothes and blew out the kerosene lantern, plunging the room into total darkness.

The rain beat a steady tattoo against the windowpane, the wind adding shrieks and moans as it whipped around the cabin's exterior. Royce stretched out on the bed, letting the sound of the storm rush over him, seep through him.

He'd told Lindsey she was a stupid fool, but it was he who was the fool . . . weak and stupid. He should have never brought her here. He should have never tempted fate . . . tempted himself. He threw an arm over his eyes, willing his body to relax.

Still, he couldn't have just left her lying unconscious in the swamp at nature's mercy. He'd had to bring her here. He'd had no other choice. So, why did he get the feeling that in bringing her home he'd made one of the biggest mistakes of his life? Why did he have the feeling that her odds of survival would have been better alone in the storm rather than in this cabin with him?

He closed his eyes, reaching for sleep, trying not to think about the woman lying in the next room, trying not to remember the sight and the feel of her soft skin as he'd undressed her. He'd forgotten how soft a woman's body could be, suppressed the memory of losing himself in lovemaking. Lindsey had made him remember, and in that memory was the torment of a thousand demons screaming damnation.

He was dreaming, and he knew it was a dream because Monica was there and he knew Monica was dead. She was in his arms, her lovely face twisted in pain and surprise. "Royce...please..." Her voice was an agonized cry. Blood. There was blood everywhere...on her, on his hands. And as he stared at his bloodstained hands he realized he was responsible. Then it was Lindsey's face before him, her eyes widened in horror.

He jerked, suddenly awake. He didn't move for a moment, allowing the last vestige of the familiar nightmare to slowly fade away. His body was bathed in a light perspiration, the dream leaving a horrid taste in his mouth. Monica had been his first mistake. He hoped the dream didn't portend Lindsey as his second.

He sat up, knowing morning approached despite the darkness outside. He'd never needed an alarm clock to awaken. His body was closely attuned to nature's timing.

The brunt of the storm had passed as he'd slept, leaving behind only a steady patter of rain against the window. He got out of bed and dressed, noting that the room had begun to fill with the gray light of a dawn obscured by clouds.

He left the bedroom, pausing in the doorway as his gaze sought her. The flickering lantern he'd left burning in the center of the table the night before played in her dark hair, pulling impish golden glints out of the rich darkness. While she'd slept, the quilt had slipped down, exposing the delicate, lace-trimmed pink bra, the creamy swell of her breasts.

His body tensed, raw energy pulsating through every vein. His need was an unchained beast, threatening to burst out of his body, rage out of control. A loud rasping noise filled his ears and he realized it was the sound of his own labored breathing.

God, it had been so long, so achingly long. He remembered the way she'd looked as he'd taken off her wet, muddied clothing. The feel of her warm skin beneath his hands, her slender length of legs, the flimsy pink lace panties that taunted and tormented him, all combined to evoke a feverish heat within him.

You could take her now, a voice whispered inside his head. *You could have her now while she's weak and vulnerable. You could still her protests with your strength, take her despite her cries.*

"No." The word whispered out of him, stilling the tormenting, taunting voice in his head. *I've got to get out of here before . . .* He didn't allow the thought to complete itself. Instead he raced for the cabin door and threw himself out into the cold, steady rain.

* * *

Lindsey awoke with a jerk, instantly appalled to realize the blanket had snaked down to her waist while she slept. She yanked it back up, at the same time sitting up and looking around.

She expelled a sigh as she realized he was nowhere to be seen. Despite the fact that the bedroom door was partially closed, she knew with a certainty he wasn't in there. His presence was absent. She was alone in the cabin.

She breathed easier and closed her eyes for a moment, thinking back over the night before. It had been horrifying. She could still feel his arms around her, his brute strength as he'd easily lifted her up and carried her to the cot. God, she'd been so afraid.

And the crying—had it only been a figment of her imagination, born of the storm and fed by the crazy stories Verla Sue had told her? She wasn't sure what frightened her more, the thought that there really could be a baby someplace out in the swamp or that she'd merely imagined the tormenting cries in her head.

She got out of bed, pleased that her headache was gone. The wound was sore to the touch, but the nausea and pounding pain had disappeared. Physically she would be fine, but she wasn't so sure about her mental well-being.

She blew out the lantern, not needing it as the room was illuminated with the gray glow of a cloud-riddled sky. Rain pattered against the roof. It would have been a cozy sound if not for where she was.

"I don't care if a hurricane roars through. I'm getting out of here today," she said aloud, buoyed by the firmness of her own voice. She anchored the quilt more firmly around her shoulders, deciding the very first thing she had to do was resume the search for her clothing. There was nothing more morale weakening than being half-naked.

She discovered them on a towel rack in the bathroom. They were still damp and muddy, but she pulled them on anyway, willing to put up with the discomfort in exchange for feeling less vulnerable.

"Now, to get out of here," she muttered, heading for the cabin door. She wasn't sure exactly when it had happened, but at some point since awakening she'd made the conscious decision that she'd rather battle the elements of the swamp than stay here one more minute with Royce.

She opened the cabin door and gasped in dismay as she looked out. She was deep in the middle of a jungle. That's the only way she could describe the cabin's surroundings. Thick, tangled underbrush and gigantic trees enveloped the area. It was a jungle that had received the brunt of the vicious storm. Trees lay tossed aside as if they were nothing more than giant toothpicks. Broken limbs hung from the trees still standing. The scene looked like the aftermath of a disaster. Beneath the wooden porch on which she stood, water swirled dark and dangerously, and she gasped once again as she saw the snout and beady eyes of an alligator.

She went back inside, slamming the cabin door and leaning against it heavily, overcome with a sense of helplessness. She'd be a fool to venture out there alone and weaponless. She had no idea where she was, no knowledge of the direction of Cindy and Remy's house. She could wander for days and never find her way out of the swamp.

Her legs trembled as she walked over to the table and sat down, her fingers playing across one of the many knife wounds in the tabletop. She couldn't leave here without Royce's help. She wouldn't attempt trying to find her way back to the house without his assistance. She was at his mercy. The thought caused a shiver of apprehension to crawl up her spine.

She thought of the strangely disturbing images she'd first had when regaining consciousness. Hands ... his hands undressing her, his eyes watching her, studying her as she lay unconscious and nearly naked. Had he touched her? Had his hand traced the curve of her breast, cupped its fullness? Surely not. Surely she would have known if his hands had lingered on her intimately. Wouldn't she?

Still, the thought that it might have happened, could have happened, filled her with a strange, languid heat. Her mouth was suddenly achingly dry and the heat of her body intensified as she thought of something else. Even if he hadn't touched her before, there was no guarantee he wouldn't as long as she remained here in his cabin. She was at his mercy. Again the words played in her mind, filling her with a horrid dread.

Her fingers once again played across the gouges in the tabletop. The knife, of course. Surely it was here someplace. At least if she had to remain here alone with Royce for any length of time, with the knife she would feel less vulnerable.

She jumped up from the table and opened first one cabinet, then another, searching for the knife she'd seen him using the night before. She found food staples and matches, extra kerosene and candles. There were canned goods and pots and pans, dishes and drinking glasses, but no knife.

She expelled a grunt of triumph as she opened a drawer and saw the silverware resting inside. As she rummaged around, disappointment swept over her when she realized the big knife wasn't there. She did find a paring knife and decided it was certainly better than nothing at all.

She'd just finished slipping the paring knife beneath the pillow on the cot when the cabin door flew open and Royce stalked in.

He was soaked from the rain, his face resembling a thundercloud as he scowled at her.

"And good morning to you, too," she muttered as he swept past her and into his bedroom, slamming the door behind him.

Lindsey looked over at her pillow, reassured by the thought of the knife resting beneath it. Even though it wasn't much of a weapon, it was something.

When he returned moments later, clad in dry clothing, Lindsey sat at the table. She was going to ask him to take her home, hope that she could appeal to whatever rational side he possessed.

"I see you found your clothes," he said, walking over to the stove and placing an iron skillet on a burner. "You hungry?"

Lindsey flushed, for a moment thrown by his seemingly sane state, so different from the dark emotions that he'd worn the night before. "Yes, as a matter of fact, I am," she answered, surprised to realize she was starving.

He opened the refrigerator door. "How about a couple of eggs?"

"Oh . . . sure," she agreed tentatively. He was certainly unpredictable, she thought, watching him warily. He grabbed the egg carton and a stick of butter from the refrigerator. It seemed strange to see him doing something as normal and mundane as preparing to fry a couple of eggs. Emboldened by the normalcy of his actions, she drew a deep breath. "Perhaps after we eat, you would be kind enough to lead me back home."

He cracked the eggs into the skillet, the sound of their sizzling filling the cabin. "I can't," he answered.

Lindsey stiffened, staring at his broad back. She tried to keep her voice as neutral as possible. "If you won't take me home, then I'll just have to find my way back by myself." She forced a bravado she didn't feel into her tone.

He turned and looked at her, his face darkly inscrutable. "You can't do that. It's a mess out there.

The water has risen and trees have fallen, blocking paths. The alligators are disoriented and dangerous and snakes are out everywhere."

"Surely you can get me home. You're the Swamp Man...you're used to all this," she said, panicked by his words. "There must be a way. Surely you can get me back to Cindy's."

"There's no way out of here until the rain stops and the water recedes." Not a flicker of emotion crossed his face, and his eyes were dark green orbs reflecting nothing. "Once the water recedes I'll have to cut new paths or clear out the old ones."

"I...I don't understand." The words crawled up Lindsey's throat with difficulty.

"Don't you?" He grinned humorlessly. "What I'm saying is that until the water recedes and I get a path cleared, you'll be my guest here."

Lindsey sat very still, letting the impact of his words sink in. His guest, or his prisoner? Her heart began an unsteady staccato in her chest and she wondered if he could hear it from where he stood across the room. She stared at him for a long moment, afraid to ask what she was about to. "How...how long will it be?"

His smile faded and a new intensity lit his eyes. "As long as it takes," he answered. Then he turned back to face the stove.

CHAPTER SEVEN

They ate in silence, the rain making the only conversation as it talked to the treetops, whispered on the roof.

The eggs were fried exactly as she liked them, crispy around the edges with mushy yellow centers. The bread he'd broiled in the oven was nicely browned and slathered with butter. She hadn't eaten since the peanut butter and jelly sandwich at noon the day before, but as she sat across from the brooding, silent man, her appetite fled.

"As long as it takes." His answer certainly hadn't breathed assurance into her chilled heart. *As long as it takes.* She would have preferred something with a little more definitive time frame, like an hour...by the end of the day.

The thought of spending the rest of the day—and more importantly, another night—in this cabin with him filled her with a sense of dread and a strange, dizzying anticipation she refused to analyze.

She looked over toward the cot, assured by the thought of the paring knife nestled beneath the pillow. She didn't stop to consider if she was capable of using a knife on somebody in self-defense. She'd find that out if and when it became necessary.

"What's the matter? You don't like the eggs?" he asked, shoving his now-empty plate aside.

"Oh, they're fine . . . very good," she hurriedly assured him, afraid of saying anything, doing anything to stir his anger that at the moment seemed to lie dormant. She bit off a piece of toast, aware of his gaze lingering on her face. She looked up at him and tried to appear as nonchalant as possible. "Exactly how long do you think it will be before the water does go down and you're able to clear a path back to Cindy's and Remy's?"

He shrugged his broad shoulders, leaning back and sweeping a strand of dark hair from his forehead. "Most likely it will be three to five days before I can get you out of here."

"Three to five days?" Lindsey forgot her decision to remain calm and gasped. "You've got to be kidding! That's impossible! Surely you can get me out of here sooner than that."

His eyes flickered with some indefinable emotion. "What's the matter, Lindsey? You don't like my little cabin in the swamp? You don't find me a hospitable host?"

"Let's just say that being here wasn't exactly written on my social calendar," she returned darkly.

His lips curved upward in what would have been a smile if it lit his eyes, but it didn't. "You have a sense of humor. Good. You'll need it to survive being here with me for the next couple of days."

He scooted his chair back and stood up, causing Lindsey's heart to flutter in anxiety. She sighed in relief as he picked up their dishes and carried them over to the sink.

As he washed the plates, Lindsey left the table and moved to sit on the edge of the cot. She felt safer, more secure with the paring knife an arm's-reach away beneath the pillow. She was so unsure of him, so afraid of his mood swings. He'd seemed almost sociable before the meal, but the pleasantness had lasted only moments.

He finished with the dishes, then disappeared into the bedroom. Seconds later he returned with his carving knife and the piece of wood he'd been working on the night before. He sat back down at the table and began working, the familiar scraping noise filling the room.

Lindsey watched him, finding him a fascinating study of harshness. Everything about him spoke of strength, and a self-containment that would have been appealing under different circumstances. He was obviously accustomed to being alone, totally self-sufficient. He was like nobody and nothing she'd ever known before.

Was he truly evil? She'd never personally met somebody who she considered the personification of evil. She supposed throughout time there had been such people ... mass murderers, sociopaths, people who made and lived by their own rules no matter who got hurt, no matter what was destroyed. Hitler was evil, Charles Manson ... yes, people could be evil. But this knowledge didn't answer the question of whether or not Royce Blanchard, the Swamp Man, was truly as bad as the people of Baton Bay seemed to believe.

She studied him again, noting the way his hands worked to stroke the knife down the length of wood with meticulous care, shaving off the bark without wounding the wood beneath. He caressed the piece of wood like a lover caressing a breast or a thigh.

She wondered how old he was. Physically he could be anywhere between the ages of twenty-five and thirty-five. There were lines at the corners of his eyes that could have been the evidence of time, or might simply speak of a life spent in the elements. Still, there was a youthful strength in his arms and shoulders and not one gray hair to hint at age.

It was his hands that fascinated her, sinewy with strength, yet long-fingered and artistic. They were capable hands she would have found attractive on anyone else, but when she looked at them all she could think about was the strength of them wrapped around her neck. Were they the hands of a man who enjoyed working with wood, or were they the tools of a madman, the weapons of his rage?

Hot hands, slowly removing her blouse, lingering over each button. Hands tugging down her jeans, moving like a gentle breeze across her stomach and down her thighs. She flushed at the sudden image and jumped up off the cot, pacing the floor of the small cabin restlessly.

The rain . . . the godforsaken rain still fell, and the scrape of Royce's knife set her teeth on edge, like fingernails raked down the surface of a chalkboard. His silence pressed in on her, further setting her nerves on edge. How could he stay quiet for so long? Didn't the man know the meaning of social conversation? How long could this taut silence continue before she screamed?

She stretched out on the cot, arms over her head, staring at the grainy patterns of the wooden ceiling. Three to five days... how was she ever going to survive?

She must have fallen asleep, for when she awoke, he'd made a fire in the stove and the kerosene lantern had been lit to ward off the invading darkness of night.

Royce had moved his chair closer to the fire. Instead of the knife, he now worked with sandpaper, rubbing it gently back and forth on the piece of wood. The glow from the lantern cast shadows on his face, creating a softening of his features. Again Lindsey was struck by how handsome he was. True, his face was one that displayed harsh features, but there was a kind of primitive beauty there as well. In the soft lighting he looked more approachable, less stern and forbidding.

She sat up, swinging her legs over the edge of the cot and stifling a yawn with the back of one hand. She watched him working for a few minutes, again noting the care he took in his work.

"What are you making?" She kept her voice soft, unassuming, afraid of his response to her attempt at conversation.

"A chair," he answered.

"A chair?" She stood up and approached where he sat, careful not to get too close. "What kind of a chair?"

"A rocking chair." He blew the dust off the wood, then ran his hand down the smooth length. "This is one of the spokes of the back," he explained.

She moved a step closer, eased by the relaxing, easy tone of his voice. "What are you going to do with it after you finish it?" she asked curiously.

"Sell it."

"Is this what you do to earn a living? You make furniture?" It didn't sound too lucrative to her.

"Among other things," he answered.

"What other things?" she persisted, wanting to know more about him. Surely the way to dispel a mystery was knowledge, she reasoned.

"Just other things." His voice held a firm note of finality, silently forbidding her to delve further.

Did you kill a woman? Did you murder your son? Are you really evil? These were the things Lindsey wanted to ask, but she was afraid to hear what the answers might be.

"It sounds like the rain is easing up," she said, moving toward the window where a gentle rain fell softly. "Maybe by tomorrow we can clear a path back to Cindy's," she added hopefully.

"Doubtful," he replied. "Even if it stopped raining this moment, it would take at least a day for the water to recede."

She walked away from the window, swallowing her disappointment at his words. At least another twenty-four hours—the thought filled her with dread. "Uh...is the shower in the bathroom functional?" she asked, finding the idea of a shower immensely appealing.

"Yes," he answered succinctly, not looking up from his handiwork.

"Would you mind if I used it?"

He looked up then and smiled sardonically. "Of course not—my house is your house."

She nodded stiffly and fled to the bathroom. Strange—she found him as disturbing in a relaxed state as she did when he radiated tension. Perhaps it was the fact that he was so unpredictable. There was no warning of when he'd change moods, shift gears and slip into the anger that never seemed very far from the surface.

She frowned as she realized the bathroom door didn't have a lock. Could she trust him—enough to undress and step into the shower?

She suddenly got a mental picture of a scene from the movie *Psycho*—the shower scene that had given her nightmares for weeks when she had been younger. Could she be certain that he wouldn't come in, his movements muted by the noisy spray of water? She shivered as she thought of that wicked knife of his slashing its way through the shower curtain.

She scoffed and began to undress. If the man wanted to ravage her body, he'd had countless chances during the last twenty-four hours. She simply had to trust the instincts that told her he wouldn't bother her. She shed the last of her clothing and fiddled with the shower controls, discovering that although the water pressure was weaker than what she was accustomed to, there seemed to be plenty of hot water.

She stepped a foot into the small enclosure, swallowing a scream as he banged on the door. Grabbing a towel, she cracked open the door a mere inch, her heart crawling up into her throat.

"Here." He shoved his hand through the crack in the door and gave her a handful of strange little leaves. "It's soap brush. If you rub the leaves between your hands beneath the water, it will lather."

Lindsey closed the door once again, looking at the pieces of plant in her hand. Soap brush? Or was it possibly some sort of aphrodisiac that would stimulate her sexuality and make it easy for him to have his way with her?

"Oh, Lindsey, honestly. Get a grip on reality," she admonished herself, stepping into the shower and beneath the spray of water. If he'd wanted to take advantage of her sexually, he'd have done it by now. Besides, he wouldn't need any plant or artificial stimuli, he was big enough and strong enough to take what he wanted no matter how hard she fought.

She rubbed the leaves together, surprised to see that they did, indeed, lather, releasing a pleasantly fresh odor she instantly identified as the scent that always surrounded Royce.

She washed her body, then her hair, lingering beneath the water, reluctant to get out and have to face him once again. How was she ever going to be able to keep her sanity until she got out of here? She thought about the broken camera lens, the incredible power it had taken to crack it in two. She thought about the stories of murder that surrounded Royce.

So far he'd seemed to maintain control. But what would happen when his control finally snapped?

Following her shower, Lindsey felt more clear-headed, more sane than she had since she'd first regained consciousness and realized she was here in his cabin. As she walked out of the bathroom she noticed he was starting dinner preparations.

She sat down on the cot and watched, admiring the efficiency of his movements, the natural grace he possessed. It was obvious he was accustomed to taking care of himself and his needs. *But man does not live on bread alone,* she thought, wondering if he ever felt the need for companionship, for love. Or had his insanity suppressed the natural need that everyone had to love and be loved?

Within minutes the cabin filled with the savory scent of meat frying. Lindsey's stomach rumbled with hunger. She'd scarcely touched the eggs that morning, and her stomach reminded her of that fact. "Is . . . is there anything I can do to help?" she asked tentatively, unsure how he would react to her offer.

"I suppose you can set the table," he answered grudgingly.

She got up from the cot, pleased to have something, anything to do. As she set the table she thought of how cozy this cabin could be under different circumstances.

The light from the fire painted the interior in gold hues and filled the air with a pleasant wood-chip scent. With the right man, it would have been intensely romantic. Or, it was easy to imagine it in the summertime with the windows flung open wide to welcome in the exotic sounds and mysterious scents of the swamp. The cabin would be a perfect place for a lovers' tryst. No telephones, no televisions, no interruptions, just wild abandoned lovemaking to fill the days and nights.

Her hands trembled as she placed their silverware and plates on the table. Her mind suddenly filled with images, erotic imaginings of strong bronzed shoulders and muscular thighs, long lean legs and large, capable hands.

She closed her eyes, able to imagine the feel of those hands stroking her body, teasing and tormenting her in loving fashion. In her mind's eye, she saw herself stroking those broad shoulders, her fingertips trailing across his flat abdomen to linger on the scar that patterned his flesh.

She sucked in a breath, horrified as she realized the naked man of her fantasy was none other than Royce.

"Are you all right?" Royce asked, setting several platters of food on the table and looking at her dispassionately.

"I'm fine," she answered, raising her hands to her flushed, heated cheeks. "I...uh...just got a pain in my head," she lied.

"Perhaps you'll feel better once you eat," he replied, although his tone made it clear he didn't care much one way or the other if she felt better.

His attitude, coupled with her momentary fantasy, stirred her resentment. Suddenly she was tired, tired of being afraid of his moods, tired of fearing the eruption of his anger. "My head wouldn't hurt if you hadn't practiced your mumbo jumbo on me."

His dark eyebrows shot up in surprise. "Mumbo jumbo?"

"Voodoo," she returned, feeling the hysteria she'd held in for so long rushing dangerously close to the surface. "I wouldn't be here now if you hadn't made that stupid wax doll and put it on my front porch. You made that tree fall and hit me in the head and knock me unconscious. You jinxed me!"

"You jinxed yourself when you didn't heed my many warnings to stay away from the swamp." He sat down at the table and motioned to the chair across from him. "Now sit down and eat before you get any more hysterical."

As angry as Lindsey was, as close to losing control as she was, she saw the warning gleam in his eyes. She took several deep breaths, then sat down across from him. "I'm not hysterical, and you owe me a new camera lens, too. You had no right to break mine." It was a final spurt of uncontrollable anger.

He smiled at her, his eyes gleaming wickedly. "Be thankful it wasn't your neck." He held her startled gaze another moment longer, then spooned several potatoes onto his plate.

The anger whooshed out of Lindsey. His words played over her, a dreadful reminder that Royce was unstable, that every moment she remained in his presence she was in danger. He was crazy, and as he'd just reminded her, he could snap her neck as easily as he'd broken her camera lens. She could almost feel his hands around her neck, see the fury in his eyes as he squeezed tightly.

"Eat," he commanded. "You'll need your strength."

Why? Why will I need my strength? she wondered wildly. *Will I have to fight him? Run from him?* Again hysteria pressed upward and she tapped it down, taking several more quick, deep breaths.

She filled her plate, taking liberal portions of the herb and buttered potatoes, the tomato and green pepper-laced corn and the chunks of lightly breaded, fried golden, but indefinable meat. She would eat, all right. She would eat lustily, heartily, get her strength up so that if she did have to fight for her life, she could.

"How do you like the meat?" he asked after a few minutes.

"It's quite good," she answered, her emotions back under tight control.

"It's gator."

If he expected her to recoil in horror, she disappointed him. Lindsey had always been an adventurous eater. She'd tried squid, octopus, snake...she wasn't afraid of trying something new. "Really?" she answered smoothly. "It's very tasty."

He scowled and went back to eating. He continued to scowl and eat in silence for the remainder of the meal.

Despite his frown, Lindsey helped him with the dishes, needing an activity of any kind. When they were finished with the cleanup, he returned to his woodworking and Lindsey restlessly paced the floor of the cabin. What on earth was she going to do to pass the time until she could leave this place? She gazed back at Royce, who sat in stoic silence. One thing she couldn't count on was stimulating conversation.

She stopped her pacing, turning toward the door as she heard a sound echoing from outside. "What's that?" she asked, moving across the wooden floor and opening the cabin door. Above the sound of the rain pattering down, she heard it once again, a curious baying. For a moment she thought it was a trick of the wind as it sang through the trees. "It . . . it sounds like dogs barking," she said more to herself than to him.

"It probably is," he replied. "Close the door, the dampness will make a chill."

She did as he asked, moving over to the window and peering out, trying to catch a glimpse of the source of the sound. It was impossible—the night darkness was an impenetrable blanket. "Maybe it's the collie I was chasing before the storm hit."

"Maybe, but he's with the ghost pack now. He won't have anything to do with humans ever again."

"Ghost pack? What's that?" She moved away from the window and gazed at him curiously.

He stopped the movement of the sandpaper and looked at her. His green eyes reminded her of a primeval forest, a place of mysteries best left alone. "A ghost pack is a bunch of dogs who run together, embracing the swamp as their home, their family. They've reverted back to the primitive rules of survival and are free from man's laws and taboos." He smiled again, the smile that held little warmth or pleasure. "Once the swamp gets hold of someone, it changes them, transforms them, making it impossible for them to return to what they once were."

Lindsey sensed both an invitation and a warning in his words. He set the knife and the piece of wood on the tabletop and stood up. He approached her slowly, his movements graceful and menacing. His gaze was a hypnotic green flame that pinned her motionless in place. Not only could she not move, she couldn't breathe.

He stopped just in front of her, his closeness making it seem like she was suddenly thrust into a dark void. The surroundings of the cabin, the sound of the rain peppering the window all faded away. Her heart pounded painfully in her chest as she got lost in his eyes.

She knew she should step back from him, but she couldn't. She couldn't think; she could do nothing but stare up at him in dreadful fascination. She was captured in the web of his nearness, caught in the heat of his gaze.

"Ah, Lindsey, you're fascinated by the swamp, aren't you?" His breath was a warm caress on her face. His hand reached out, a finger touching the side of her nose, moving down her cheek and tracing her jawline from her ear to her chin. She fought the irrational impulse to turn her head, capture his finger in her mouth, taste his flesh.

He stepped closer to her, his broad chest against the tips of her breasts. She could feel his heart beat . . . or was it her own, pounding with the rhythm of thick, heated blood. And to her horror, she felt her nipples rising, as if reaching out for the firmness of his chest. The air was full of tension and danger, and a barely contained passion that terrified yet mesmerized her.

His hand reached out and tangled in the back of her hair. With an insistent tug, he pulled her head backward, tilting her face upward, her lips only inches from his.

"It's the darkness that first pulls you in, mystifies and fascinates," he breathed as his lips descended on hers.

His mouth blazed, consuming her in flames of desire she hadn't realized had been simmering. She tasted his power, felt the swirling evocation of his dark soul calling to hers. There was a hunger in his lips, a devouring hunger that wrenched an answering in her.

She suddenly knew the reason why throughout time women had been attracted to dangerous men. Her fear for her life, her fear for her very soul, fled in the presence of his mastery. The utter maleness, the raw sensuality, the pure eroticism of the kiss all combined to create a heady desire that made her dizzy, compelled her to consider what it would be like if he made love to her, consumed her with the fire of his passion and depth of his madness. And as he deepened the kiss, his tongue touching first the edge of her teeth, then exploring deeper within, she felt herself responding, realized there was a madness in her answering to the call of his.

The kiss seemed to last an eternity, his mouth evoking responses in her that both frightened and stimulated her. Thought was no longer possible. She could only feel, only accept the craziness he stirred within. He was no longer the dreaded Swamp Man, and she no longer Lindsey Witherspoon. They were merely pawns in a game that had no rules.

She could feel his heart against her own, beating an unsteady rhythm of wildness. She felt a vague tremor coursing through his body, and in some distant part of her mind it registered that he was as aroused as she.

He slowly removed his mouth from hers, his hand still tangled in her hair. His eyes burned intensely into hers and still she couldn't move, couldn't look away. "Oh, yes, you're drawn to the darkness, aren't you, Lindsey?" His breath stirred her hair, fanned her face.

He placed his hand on the curve of her breast, where her heart beat in resounding unsteadiness. "Be careful, Lindsey. People who become fascinated with the swamp and enter into its dark center never really are the same again."

His words, coupled with the intimate touch of his hand on her breast, finally broke the spell she had been under and she stumbled back from him, needing some distance from his overwhelming closeness.

"You're talking nonsense," she scoffed uneasily, waves of heat still coursing through her body. "The only fascination I have for the swamp at the moment is an intense desire to get out of it."

He laughed then, a deep-throated chuckle that did nothing to make her feel better. "Then perhaps you aren't as foolish as I think," he replied. He walked back over to the table and picked up his wood and sandpaper. "Blow out the lantern before you go to sleep," he said as he disappeared into the bedroom, closing the door behind him.

CHAPTER EIGHT

Lindsey stood beneath the shower flow, wishing, hoping the water could wash away the lingering imprint of Royce's hands on her, hoping her own strange feelings would disappear beneath an onslaught of water. She'd tossed and turned all night, her blood roaring in her ears and her insides quivering with despair. It was crazy, the whole thing was crazy and frightening.

For a moment, for just a brief moment while his lips had been on hers the night before, she'd been afraid that he would sweep her into his arms, carry her into the bedroom and take her.

But it wasn't this that caused despair to wing its way through her body. What made her afraid was that for just a moment, for just a single, insane moment, that was exactly what she had wanted him to do. She'd wanted to feel his power. She'd answered the call of his madness and it was this that scared the hell out of her.

Even now, his taste lingered on her lips. It was the taste of mystery and tightly leashed passion. She could still feel the heat from his hand on her breast. Just thinking about it made her knees grow weak, and she leaned against the wall of the shower enclosure.

She reached up and touched the cut on her fore-head, wondering if perhaps something important had been scrambled by the blow from the tree. How else to explain that she had responded to Royce...the Swamp Man?

She plunged her head beneath the spray of water, hoping her strange feelings would disappear down the drain, washed away forever.

She'd awakened minutes earlier to face another morning of gloom. Although the rain had stopped sometime during the night, the skies still were over-cast. Royce was gone, hopefully out working to clear a path that would lead her home.

As she dried off, she thought again of that moment in his arms when her sanity had fled and she'd suc-cumbed to the hot demand of his mouth. A momen-tary weakness, she reasoned, a weakness brought on by a vicious blow to her head and her disorientation in these surroundings. It really had nothing to do with desire, rather it was created by fear and the anxiety of the unknown.

She thought of what he'd said to her the night be-fore, his whispered words about the pull of the dark-ness of the swamp. He might just as well have been talking about himself.

She sighed, shoving thoughts of Royce from her mind. She picked up her clothes from the floor, dreading the thought of putting on the mud-splattered jeans and grimy blouse yet again. She longed for something clean to wear. She frowned, thinking of the closet in Royce's bedroom. Although anything of his would be big, at least it would be better than having to climb back into her own dirty clothes. Did she dare use something of his?

She quickly wrapped the towel around her and cautiously opened the bathroom door, listening for a moment, assuring herself he hadn't returned while she'd been showering.

Hearing nothing, she quickly scampered into the bedroom and pulled open the closet door. Shirts and jeans hung neatly in a row. The shirts were mostly long-sleeved chambray and flannel, although there were several short-sleeved white T-shirts. She bypassed these and pulled out one of the chambray shirts, buttoning it up and rolling up the sleeves. Although the shirt threatened to swallow her up, it was soft and clean-smelling.

She pulled down a pair of jeans and tugged them on, the waist and hips big and the legs requiring several roll-ups. She started to close the closet door, but paused a moment, her attention captured by a pale pink lacy sleeve. Curiously she shoved Royce's clothing aside, gasping in surprise as she discovered several feminine articles of clothing. The pink lacy sleeve belonged to a blouse. There were also several more tops, a pair of jeans, a denim skirt and two sundresses. She checked the size on one of the dresses. A size bigger than what Lindsey wore.

She closed the door thoughtfully. What on earth was Royce doing with women's clothes in his closet? Who did they belong to?

She went back into the bathroom and picked up her own dirty things. She carried them into the kitchen and placed them in the sink. She would wash them out and hang them near the stove and hopefully they would dry quickly.

As she washed them, her mind whirled with questions. *Maybe Royce is a cross-dresser.* A giggle bubbled to her lips at this absurd thought. The giggle slowly died as she realized she was subconsciously skirting the obvious answer. It seemed a natural assumption to make that the clothing belonged to the female scientist Verla had told her about, the woman who had entered into the swamp and never come out. She shivered as she took the thought a step further...the same woman it was rumored that Royce had killed.

She wrung out her clothes and placed them across the back of one of the chairs, then moved the chair closer to the stove. A sick feeling moved around in the pit of her stomach as she thought again of the pretty pink blouse, the feminine sundresses that hung in the closet. Did they belong to a dead woman? Lindsey had heard that murderers, especially the really sick ones, liked to keep souvenirs of their victims. Were those clothes Royce's souvenirs?

She whirled around with a gasp as the cabin door opened and he walked in. He stared at her for a moment, his dark gaze making her throat grow dry. "I...uh...I hope you don't mind, I borrowed some of your clothes. Mine were dirty so I rinsed them out and..." Her voice trailed off beneath the intensity of his gaze.

"There are some things that would fit you better," he said, moving across the room to stand in front of the stove.

"Oh, no, these are fine, just fine," Lindsey hurriedly assured him, appalled at the thought of wearing one of those feminine items of clothing...clothing that possibly belonged to a dead woman. "Are you hungry? I could fix you something," she offered tentatively. She sensed tension in him and watched him warily.

"I'm not hungry." A muscle pulsed in his jaw, knotting and reknotting with rhythmic regularity.

Lindsey's nose twitched, smelling danger in the air. She silently slid across the floor and sank down onto the cot near the pillow and the small knife hidden beneath.

Royce went into the bedroom, coming back out with a new piece of wood and the wicked, sharp knife. He sat at the kitchen table and began to work.

Lindsey curled up on the bed in an attempt to make herself as invisible as possible. She had the distinct feeling that he was on the verge of a rage, and she didn't want to be on the receiving end if he lost control. She smelled the sulfur scent of hell's fire ready to erupt.

The minutes crept by with excruciating slowness. Boredom made her restless, but fear kept her from fidgeting. She tried to keep her eyes off Royce, but again and again she found herself warily watching him.

He didn't caress the wood, rather his knife tore down the bark, unmindful of the soft wood beneath. His body was taut, radiating a tension she found threatening.

Lindsey suppressed a shiver, averting her gaze from him, trying to think of something—anything—pleasant. She thought longingly of the half gallon of caramel ripple ice cream sitting in Cindy's refrigerator. What she wouldn't give for a bite of the soothing dessert this minute.

She looked at the wall, thinking of her camera, still sitting by the chaise longue near the pool. It was probably ruined, completely waterlogged. The pictures she'd taken before the storm had erupted were probably gone as well. Oh well, maybe when she got out of here she would buy a new camera and go to the Grand Canyon or Yellowstone National Park and take photographs. One thing was certain. Once she got out of here she was never coming back. She'd had enough swamp to last a lifetime.

She sighed and watched Royce as he carved. Is this the way he spends most of his days? she wondered. All alone with nobody to talk to? No wonder he was crazy. She'd only been here a little more than twenty-four hours and already she felt half-loony.

The throb in Royce's jawline intensified, and Lindsey watched in fascination as the muscles knotted beneath the skin. The silence between them grew, stretched taut and uncomfortable.

"Must you stare at me?" He suddenly exploded, driving the knife point into the tabletop and turning to glare at her.

Lindsey swallowed a squeak of surprise and glared back at him. "Well, I'm sorry. There really isn't much else to do. I assume all your magazine subscriptions have lapsed," she replied sarcastically as her own control snapped. She was tired of sitting quietly, tired of being afraid. After all, this was all his fault. He was the one who'd brought her here.

He jerked up out of his chair and stalked across the room where he opened a cabinet and withdrew several books. "Here, maybe these will keep you occupied," he said, throwing them down on the foot of the cot, then sitting back down.

Lindsey picked up the books with interest. All three of them were textbooks on swamps and marshlands. She opened the first one, immediately intrigued as she read the introductory text.

For the next couple of hours she pored over the first textbook, which covered the Okefenokee Swamp. She was fascinated with the history of the area, the first accounts of the people who'd chosen to settle there. She was pleased that although the photos in the book were good, they didn't hold a candle to the ones she had taken and shown to Verla Sue.

What fascinated her most was the handwritten notes in the margins of the book. Jotted in pencil, some of them nearly illegible, many made comparisons between this particular swamp and the Okefenokee. She was surprised to see Royce's name in the margins. *Ask*

Royce. Check this out with R. His name and initial appeared with regular frequency.

She looked up as Royce scooted his chair back and stood. She watched as he fed the stove with several logs. He then busied himself at the refrigerator, apparently preparing to make dinner. She looked at her watch, surprised to see that it was almost four o'clock. She'd read most of the day away. She closed the book and stretched.

The air in the cabin had changed in the passing hours. The tension had dissipated and the muscle that had been jumping in Royce's jaw was still. The fire glowed through the grate on the stove, spilling golden light around the room.

Lindsey got up off the cot and went to the cabinet where the dishes were kept. She offered him a smile and, to her surprise, he smiled back. It was a small one, and the gesture looked stiff, as if his lips were unaccustomed to curving upwards, but it was a smile, nevertheless. It made him appear softer, a little vulnerable, and Lindsey again found herself marveling at his attractiveness.

"Thanks for the books. They're fascinating," she said as she set the table.

"At least it's something for you to do while you're here," he replied, setting a pot of what appeared to be some sort of stew on a burner.

"I'm really enjoying them, especially the part that talked about how swamps were settled."

"You mean by all the outlaws and rebels who refused to live in a rigid, hypocritical society?" His smile was now sardonic.

"That's pretty much what the book inferred," she admitted. She pulled out a chair and sat down at the table. "Have you always lived here in the swamp?"

He nodded. "Born and raised here just like my mother before me. I come from a long line of swamp-dwellers."

"Where did they all go? From what I heard in town, you're the only one living here."

His dark eyebrows quirked upward. "Do you believe everything people tell you?"

Lindsey flushed, remembering the stories she'd heard about him. "Not everything," she answered slowly. "I don't believe that your father was the devil."

He stared at her, startled for a moment, then threw back his head and laughed. It was a rusty sound, as if laughter had rarely made its way to his lips. Still, it was not an unpleasant sound. "You mean, you don't believe that the master of darkness himself climbed up from the depths of hell for a passionate interlude with my mother?" He turned and stirred the stew, his back to her. "My father was a revenuer who came to the swamp to catch moonshiners. He caught my mother instead, caught her for a night, then was gone with the morning sun."

There was something in his words, an emptiness, an echo of a little boy lost, that made Lindsey want to reach out to him. She fought the impulse, knowing instinctively that if she showed him any tenderness it would anger him. And she feared his anger more than anything. "It must have been hard, growing up without a father," she finally said.

"It wasn't so bad." He turned and looked at her once again, his eyes glowing in the firelight. "The swamp is my family. It taught me to survive."

"But there's more to life than survival," she objected softly. "Don't you ever get lonely? Don't you ever have the desire for friends? Companionship?"

"And who would be my friend?" His face twisted, the handsome features obliterated beneath a mask of suppressed rage, and his voice was savage. "In Baton Bay, the parents don't tell their children stories of the bogeyman. They frighten them with tales of the Swamp Man. They whisper horror in my name, they cross themselves when I pass them on the street. I'm their nightmare. I make them cry out in the night. Who would have me for a friend?"

"I would." The words slipped out of her unbidden, an automatic response to the torment she heard in his voice.

He snorted derisively. "Let's eat," he said, ending the conversation by slamming the stewpot on the table.

Again their meal was eaten in silence, Lindsey's mind filled with his bitter words. Questions and assessments whirled around and around. Was he the monster that the people of Baton Bay believed him to be, or was he simply a man who'd been tormented by the cruel taunts of townspeople who feared him because he was different from them? There were still so many questions about him, so many mysteries left to solve.

There was the rumor that he'd killed the woman, and Lindsey was sure this rumor was founded in something more substantial than the fears of a town full of superstitious people.

She remembered his hands wrapped around her neck, the threat that had radiated from his eyes. She could almost feel the heat of his hands on her hair, caressing as he told her how pretty the other one had been ... until he had buried her. Who was the other woman? What, exactly, had she been doing here in the swamp and how had she died?

The questions nagged and picked at her brain, demanding answers. But she was afraid of what the answers might be, afraid not only for her physical safety but also the safety of her soul.

No, the best thing to do was keep the conversation light and pleasant, do nothing to stir the rage he carried in his heart, then get the hell out of here as soon as possible.

After dinner, Royce once again sat at the table working with a piece of wood. The muscle was back, ticking in his jaw with the regularity of a time bomb ticking to detonation.

Lindsey paced the cabin, too restless to read, tired of sitting. The tension was back in the air, and she was aware of his dark gaze lingering on her as she paced back and forth.

She finally stopped at the window, staring out at the wildness beyond. Twilight stole in, barely discernible as it darkened the gloom of the day. She moved to the front door and stepped out onto the porch, breathing in the pungent odor of greenery and lingering rain. Noise surrounded her, the low croaking of a chorus of frogs, the slap of a fish against the surface of the water, the scurrying of an animal in the nearby underbrush. Bats swooped down, eating insects from the tree leaves and brush.

Despite the fact that she knew the waters were filled with vicious alligators and dangerous snakes, there was a beautiful tranquillity that seeped into her heart and made her relax. It would be easy for her to learn to love this place. She'd known it from the moment she'd arrived at Cindy's and looked toward the swamp. It had drawn her like no place she had ever been.

She tensed as she heard the door open behind her. Immediately the frogs quieted and a pervading silence filled the area, letting her know that Royce had stepped out onto the porch behind her. "Don't worry, I haven't run off," she said, wondering if that's why he had come out, to check on her.

"I wasn't worried. If you did leave, you wouldn't get far alone." His breath warmed the back of her neck, letting her know he was standing very close.

"It's beautiful out here," she said softly, as if afraid her voice would spoil the quiet of the evening.

"Beautiful, but dangerous," he agreed, his voice also soft. "There's a legend about a singing snake, a black snake that sings the most compelling lullaby ever heard by human ears.'' His deep voice was like soft velvet, wrapping around her like a cloak. ''Legend has it that the singing snake is partnered with a deadly rattlesnake. The magical snake sings a siren song, luring a human near, then the rattler strikes out and kills the man or woman who followed the seductive call.''

''That's a horrible legend,'' Lindsey breathed.

''Perhaps, but it epitomizes the essence of this place.''

And you, Lindsey added mentally. ''The swamp doesn't have a monopoly on danger. There's danger everywhere,'' she scoffed. ''In Washington, D.C., people get mugged and murdered every day. They get hit by cars and fall down stairs. Then there's air pollution.''

He laughed, the deep, rusty sound washing over her with welcomed warmth. ''D.C....is that where you're from?''

It was the first personal question he'd asked her. It was a good sign, and she turned to look at him. ''I was a secretary and personal assistant to a man who was in politics.'' She noticed that Royce's features were slowly melting away into the encroaching darkness of the night.

''So, what brought you here?''

Lindsey turned back around to face the swamp, reaching back into memories from what seemed a lifetime ago. ''My boss was also my fiancé, and when I found him in bed with another woman I not only quit the job, but also the man.''

"Ah, politics." His voice filled with amusement. "Such is the stuff that keeps a man in the swamp."

"What happened to all the other people who used to live here?" Lindsey asked curiously.

"When I was younger I had several aunts and uncles who lived nearby. They're all gone now, moved away or dead."

For a moment they stood in silence, looking out at the area that held such beauty and mystery. She tried to imagine what it had been like for him as a child, growing up in the primitive surroundings, learning the nuances and elements of nature on an intimate level. It was somehow a romantic notion, and she realized that the swamp was as firmly entrenched in Royce's soul as he was in the swamp's depths.

She looked up in surprise as the moon broke through the clouds, bathing the area in a soft light that illuminated the darkness and transformed the Spanish moss into shiny silver curtains. She caught her breath, awed at the ethereal effect.

All thought fled Lindsey's mind as her gaze caught on something amid the trees. She squinted, gasping as she saw a figure in a billowy white dress, long hair flowing down her back as she ran from tree to tree.

"Royce!" Lindsey reached behind her and grabbed his hand, pulling him up to stand directly next to her. "There's somebody out there." She pointed to the trees, cursing silently as the moon skirted behind thick clouds, extinguishing the illumination.

"There's nothing there. You're imagining things," Royce replied.

"There *is* somebody there," Lindsey protested vehemently. "It was a woman." She looked up where the dark clouds completely swallowed the moon. "Damn, where's the moon?" She redirected her focus back to the spot where she'd seen the woman. There was nothing there now, only darkness. "She was there, I know she was, and if she came into the swamp then there must be a way for me to get out." She cupped her hands to her mouth. "Hello!" she yelled. "Hello? Who's there?"

She gasped as Royce grabbed her by the shoulders and spun her around to face him. "Lindsey, there's nobody there. Nobody." His fingertips dug painfully into her shoulders and his eyes blazed with an intensity that frightened her. "Your imagination is running wild. There's nobody there. I was out in the swamp this morning. Trees are down everywhere. There's no way in and there's no way out." He released his grip on her shoulders. "I'm going inside."

He turned and went back into the cabin, leaving her alone on the porch. Lindsey looked back at the place where she could have sworn she saw the woman. The moon peeked out from the clouds, once again casting light to the ground. Nothing. There was nothing there. Had it just been her imagination? It had seemed so real. She could still see in her mind the way the woman's gown had billowed behind her as she ran, the way her hair had flowed with her movements. Why would she imagine such a thing?

She leaned against the railing, a dull headache starting to pound in her temples. And if she really wasn't imagining it, if the woman was really real, then who was she and where had she come from? Could Lindsey trust Royce when he said all the paths were blocked? Or was he merely telling her that to keep her here with him for some purpose only his insanity could understand?

Real or unreal, the woman was there no longer. With a sigh, Lindsey pushed herself off the railing and went into the cabin. Royce had disappeared into the bedroom, but he had lit the kerosene lantern in the center of the table.

Lindsey placed a log in the stove, standing near the heat, hoping it could pierce through to where a chill gripped her heart. She shivered, rubbing her upper arms, wondering if the space around her heart would ever be warm again. The chill that pervaded her body had nothing to do with the damp night air, rather it was a response to Royce and her growing fear for her own sanity.

"I know I saw a woman out there," she whispered aloud. But even though the words were spoken with conviction, she just wasn't sure. In fact, the longer she stayed here in this cabin, the less sure she was about anything.

If the woman had been a figment of her imagination, why that particular image? If she was going to fantasize images, why not a whole army come to rescue her? Why not a helicopter to lift her out of here? At least a Weed Eater to help clear a path. A giggle spilled from her lips, and she realized hysteria was once again crawling up her throat.

She blew out the lantern and stepped out of the jeans, then crawled beneath the covers on the cot. Surely by tomorrow night she would be back at Cindy's and this would all just seem like a bad dream. She closed her eyes and allowed her mind to go blank, seeking the comfort of dreamless sleep.

She opened her eyes, instantly realizing she'd been soundly sleeping but something had awakened her. She didn't move for a long moment, her heart pounding erratically. Then she heard it, the baby crying. The cries rose and fell, carried through the swamp on a phantom wind.

"Shut up, you aren't real," she whispered, slapping her hands over her ears in despair. Still the sound intruded—fitful and relentless, the child's unhappiness pierced through Lindsey's heart.

"Stop it," she hissed, plugging her ears with her fingers. But the noise continued, sometimes barely discernible, then rising in pitch and volume.

She pulled herself out of bed. *It is real,* she thought. *It's as real as I am. Why was Royce lying about it?*

When she'd first heard the cries, she was willing to concede it might have been the wind shrieking through the trees. Even the other night, in the midst of the storm, when she'd opened Royce's window, it might have again been storm-related. But tonight there was no wind, no rain to blame it on. There was a baby crying out there, and it was as real as her standing here.

She went over to the window and stared out. The moonlight was bright, the dark clouds having moved on to distant places. However, despite the illumination, there was nothing to see.

As the sound once again increased in volume, Lindsey made a decision. She went over to Royce's bedroom door and cracked it open. The moonlight spilled fully into his window, bathing him in its golden light.

"Royce?" she whispered tentatively.

He sat up at the sound of his name, his eyes glittering iridescently. "What do you want?"

"I hear it again...the baby. Listen," she instructed. For a moment she stood completely still, straining to hear what she'd been hearing so clearly for the past few minutes. She heard nothing. "I know I heard it." She moved over to the window next to his bed and cracked it open. "If you'll just listen for a minute you'll hear it, too."

"Go to bed, Lindsey." His voice sounded weary. "You're overtired. There's nothing there. You need to sleep."

Lindsey's control snapped. "Don't patronize me," she exclaimed, clutching desperately to her anger. It was the easiest emotion to accept. She was tired of her fear, and scared to death of the indefinable emotion his naked chest evoked. Anger was good, clean, and she clung to it with fevered intensity. "Dammit, why do you persist in telling me there is no baby when I know perfectly well there is!"

"Lindsey, I'm warning you...get out of here and go back to bed." His voice was a growl of barely contained anger. There was a new tension in the air, one that caused the air in her lungs to escape with a hiss. His eyes spilled a sensual threat she found more terrifying than his hands around her neck.

"Or what?" she whispered, losing all control, beyond fear, surpassing rationality. She froze suddenly, realizing by the look on his face that she had pushed him over the edge.

With the swiftness of a striking snake, he reached out and captured her arm, pulling her down to him. With a frightened cry she stumbled onto the bed, falling across his naked chest. His mouth claimed hers in hungry demand, kissing her with a passion, spinning her into a vortex of emotion she couldn't escape.

The worst part was, she didn't want to escape. She wanted to fall into his madness, lose herself in his arms. She didn't fight against him; instead she melted into his heat, letting the insanity claim her totally.

She responded without thought, fueled only by his hunger and her own. Her hands splayed against the width of his chest, feeling the sinewy muscles beneath the warm skin. She knew with a certainty that this was where they had been heading since they'd first met, this moment with his mouth devouring hers, his hands hotly stroking up beneath the chambray shirt.

She knew he was aroused to fever pitch, she felt it in his heartbeat, in the trembling of his body. His arousal fed hers and she moaned deep within her throat.

He stiffened against her, wrenching his mouth free from hers. He released his hold on her, his face twisted in savage bitterness. "Get out of here, Lindsey," he said hoarsely, physically shoving her away from him. "Get out of here before I do something I'll be sorry for."

She stumbled to her feet next to the bed, confused, frightened by the almost inhuman glint in his eyes, the angry slash of his lips. "Get out," he raged. "I wanted Monica and now she's dead. If you don't get out of this room right now, I can't be responsible for what might happen to you."

Lindsey didn't wait to see what the consequences would be if she lingered. She turned and ran.

CHAPTER NINE

Had Lindsey been able to, she would have run for miles. As it was, she ran into the next room, her chest heaving as if she'd just run a marathon. Her skin burned and prickled where his hands had touched her, but an icy knot of fear lay heavy in the pit of her stomach.

She sank down on the bed, her legs refusing to hold her any longer. She pulled her knees up to her chest, wrapping her arms around them, trying to control the shivers that jerked her body convulsively.

His face... She would never forget the savage intensity of his face. His eyes had radiated a haunting torment, his face twisted with a cancerous anger. "I wanted Monica and now she's dead." His words played and replayed across her mind, and she tightened her grip around her knees in an attempt to stop the shakes.

Although his words to her had implied threat, she'd sensed an underlying deep despair that was out of her realm of understanding. Who was Monica? Exactly how had she died? Had Royce killed her? There was a part of Lindsey's brain that rebelled at this thought. But as she thought of the all-consuming power of his anger, she had to accept this possibility. Fear once again raced through her, hot and cold, dreadful with implication.

How long could she stay here and trust him to maintain control? How long could she remain in this cabin and not lose her mind? She was already teetering on the edge, seeing women who were not there, hearing phantom baby cries, feeling a white-hot desire for a man who might possibly be an insane murderer.

This thought made her shivering stop and a warm heat suffuse her body. There had been something in his kiss, in his touch, that had transcended the mere physical act. It was as if his spirit had reached deep within her and for a moment taken possession of her soul. It had been like nothing she'd ever experienced before, and it both frightened and excited her.

Her fingertips trembled as she brought one hand up to touch her lips. His kiss had been so devouring, holding the passion and hunger of a man of great depth. What frightened her more than anything was that for a brief moment she had descended into that depth and lost herself in the darkness that resided there.

She stared at his bedroom door. He'd wanted Monica and now Monica was dead. He wanted Lindsey and it was only his tight control that had saved her from whatever fate Monica had suffered. How long could he manage to maintain control? Dear God, she had to get out of here before everything exploded.

She slid down on the cot, reaching beneath the pillow and feeling for the paring knife. Her fingers curled securely around the handle and she released a shuddering sigh.

She awoke to the sun cascading warmth and light into the room. It was like a beacon of hope, washing away the previous night's despair and filling Lindsey with optimism. Surely today Royce would get a path cleared and lead her back to Cindy and Remy's house.

As she got off the cot, the paring knife rattled to the floor. She stared down at it for a long moment and as her mind filled with thoughts of Royce, the width of his shoulders, the strength of his muscles, she realized the weapon was pitiful and would probably be completely useless against him.

Besides, she had a gut feeling that she would find it impossible to stab the blade into a vital organ no matter what the circumstances.

She picked up the small knife and put it back into the drawer where she'd found it, aware that in doing so she was placing her life in the hands of fate and Royce.

She checked her clothing by the wood-burning stove, finding it still too damp to put on, then went into the bathroom and washed her face.

Her wound had scabbed over and begun the healing process. The redness around it had vanished, and it wasn't as tender to the touch.

She ran her hands through her hair, trying to finger-comb the tangles out. *Surely Royce has a hairbrush someplace,* she thought, looking around the bathroom. But there was no brush to be found. Perhaps in his bedroom, she reasoned.

She opened his bedroom door cautiously, although she was pretty sure he was gone. She went directly to the top drawer of the wooden dresser, expelling a triumphant sigh as she spied a brush on top of a bunch of papers. She pulled it out and quickly ran it through her hair, closing her eyes as she felt the tangled mass returning to soft curls. She started to put the brush back when she saw a particular piece of paper that looked interesting.

Pulling it out, she read it and gasped. A marriage certificate. The paper was an official document certifying that one Monica Peterson had married Royce Blanchard almost two years before.

Lindsey stared at the paper in shocked surprise. None of the stories she'd heard about Royce included his marriage. Why didn't everyone know he'd married this Monica? She looked down at the bottom of the paper and realized the answer. Royce and Monica had been married not in Baton Bay, but rather in New Orleans. That explained why nobody in Baton Bay knew. New Orleans was almost a hundred miles from this little burg.

She placed the document back in the drawer, carefully putting the hairbrush back on top of it, and left Royce's bedroom, her mind still whirling.

She sat at the table, head in her hands, as she tried to digest exactly what the knowledge she'd just gained meant. Monica Peterson was probably the woman scientist who had entered the swamp several years before. The clothes in Royce's closet were hers, as were the books Royce had given Lindsey to read. Monica and Royce had married. Had there been a baby? And had something horrible happened, causing Royce to kill both his wife and his son? This scenario was even more horrifying than any she'd previously heard. It was also a scenario that refused to compute with her perception of the man who'd kissed her the night before, the man who so far had done nothing to harm her. She reached back into her memory, trying to pluck out every single thing Verla Sue had told her about Royce. Nothing that she remembered gave her any comfort.

She raised her head, aware of a sound coming from outside, a rhythmic, resounding noise like someone chopping wood. Royce... he must be out there working to clear away the fallen trees.

Once again hope buoyed through her. She got up from the table and went to the front door, opening it and stepping out onto the porch. The sunshine greeted her, like a welcoming fire on a cold, wintry night. She raised her face to it, letting its warmth bathe her, hoping its heat would penetrate to the coldness that still resided inside her chest.

She looked around, wishing she had her camera as she studied the surroundings. The greens and browns of the trees and brush were so intense, as if the rain had heightened the hues to a surreal intensity. Once again the chopping sound resumed, coming from a nearby area to her left. She decided to follow the sound, see what kind of progress Royce was making.

The water beneath the porch stairs had receded, although the ground was muddy. She jumped from the bottom step to a patch of trampled grass. If felt good to be outside, breathing the clean, rain-scented air. She paused a moment, reveling in the sensations of fresh air and sunshine. She stepped over a fallen tree limb, following the sound of thudding into the underbrush.

She saw him about a hundred yards in front of her, applying an ax to a thick tree trunk that blocked the small path. The ax swung up over his head and down, creating the echoing thud she'd heard.

For a moment she merely watched. A primitive man battling natural elements. He'd taken his shirt off, and his bronzed muscles rippled and danced with every overhead swing of the ax. Again Lindsey wished she had her camera. There was something so atavistic about the scene, as if it weren't the twentieth century but hundreds of years before and Royce were one of the original swamp dwellers carving a home from the wilderness.

She approached him noisily, aware that the last thing she wanted to do was sneak up on a man with an ax in his hands. She'd just about reached where he was working when she saw a strange-looking lump lying nearby. Cautiously, she moved closer, a cry strangling in her throat as she realized it was the body of a fawn. Its head had been crushed. "Oh, God," she gulped, stumbling sideways, afraid she was going to be ill.

Royce threw down the ax and moved to her side. "I found it beneath that tree trunk," he explained. He crouched down and placed a hand gently on the flank of the dead animal. "Poor thing was probably running scared in the storm and was hit by the falling tree." His hand caressed the mottled hide. "There is no justice in the swamp...even the most innocent can become a victim."

"What...what are you going to do with it?" Lindsey asked.

"Bury it so the scavengers don't get to it." He stood up again. "What are you doing out here, anyway?"

Lindsey shrugged, keeping her eyes carefully averted from the hapless fawn. "The sun was shining and I felt like getting out of the cabin. I thought I'd come and see how you were progressing."

"Slowly," he answered. "If you are going to walk around the swamp, make sure you always keep the cabin in your sights. I've got enough work to do without having to hunt for you." His voice was gruff, and he turned around and picked up his ax. He set to work once again, and Lindsey started picking her way back to the cabin. As she walked, she thought of the way Royce's hand had lingered on the dead animal... gently, tenderly, as if he mourned the fawn's death. He was going to bury it so no scavengers would get to it. Were these the actions of a man who was capable of killing his wife and child? She was so confused. Who was the real Royce Blanchard?

She reached the bottom step of the porch, deciding she wasn't ready to go back into the airless confines of the cabin. Surely she could explore just a little, keeping in mind Royce's warning to keep the cabin in her sights.

She chose a path that looked well-trampled, carefully walking around the areas that were most muddy. As she worked her way deeper into the undergrowth, she became aware of the rather unpleasant scent of decaying vegetation. Overhead branches effectively blocked out the sunlight, a damp chill working its way up her spine. She paused a moment, gazing with interest at a patch of strange-looking moss on the side of a tree. Again a prickly feeling raced up her back, raising the hairs on the back of her neck. She twirled around, distinctly feeling that someone was staring at her. She gazed around the wooded area, seeing nothing, nobody.

"Just call me the Queen of Paranoia," she muttered, turning her attention back to the moss.

"Go home." The voice drifted on the wind, faint and otherworldly.

Lindsey spun around once again, her heart thudding painfully in her chest. "Who... who said that?" she breathed.

"Stay away from him."

Lindsey froze, trying to discern where the voice had come from. Somebody was here in the woods with her, unless the trees were talking to her, and if that was the case she wished somebody would throw her a pair of ruby slippers and let her find her way home.

Seconds ticked by. A mosquito buzzed around her head, perspiration trickled beneath her hair, but she didn't move, didn't blink an eye.

Her persistence was rewarded as a woman suddenly ran from the cover of one tree trunk to hide behind another. It was the same woman she'd seen the evening before. She wore a white, billowing gown and long, dark hair fell down her back. "Hey, wait a minute," Lindsey yelled, running in the direction of the woman. She cursed as her feet slipped and slid on the wet moss, and she saw the woman moving ahead of her.

"Hey, wait, I just want to talk to you," Lindsey yelled, running desperately to catch up with the fleeing woman. She jumped over exposed roots, tore her way through tangled brush, never looking away from the figure that ran in front of her.

A stitch grabbed her side and her breath came in painful gasps as she tried to increase her speed. But the woman was fleet of foot and obviously knew the area much better than Lindsey. Lindsey gasped in surprise as her foot tangled in a vine and she tumbled to the ground, banging her knee painfully against a fallen tree limb.

She looked up just in time to see the white-garbed woman pause and look back at her. Shock ripped through Lindsey as she realized the woman was not young. Her face was lined with wrinkles. Gray hair coiled around her face, wild as Medusa's hair of snakes. Her eyes slashed through the distance to bore into Lindsey's. "Go home before you destroy him," she said.

"Wait," Lindsey exclaimed, struggling to her feet, but the woman turned and ran, disappearing into the woods.

"Damn," Lindsey expelled, experimentally putting weight on her leg. Her knee throbbed painfully, but it seemed to work okay.

She limped to where she had last seen the woman standing. It was useless to try to follow her into the thick woods. All Lindsey would accomplish would be to get hopelessly, helplessly lost. "Damn, damn, double damn," she spat, sliding down to sit at the foot of a tree, rubbing her knee with one hand.

Was she real? Or was I chasing a figment of my imagination? Did I really hear her speak, or was it merely an extension of my hallucination?

Lindsey groaned and stood up once again. She leaned against the tree, trying to catch her breath. The woman had been right here, standing in this very spot when she had paused and looked right at Lindsey.

Frustration bubbled around inside of Lindsey. She'd been so close to the woman, she'd seen the wrinkles that crisscrossed her face, the mole that decorated the side of her mouth, the eyes that had glared so malevolently.

Lindsey frowned as her eyes lit on something bright yellow lying at the side of the tree. What was this? She bent down and picked it up, staring blankly at what she held in her hand. A rattle. A child's rattle. Bright yellow plastic in the shape of a smiling daisy, with little beads inside.

"She was real," Lindsey breathed. "She was real and she dropped this as she ran." Lindsey laughed aloud, realizing that if there was a rattle, then there had to be a baby, and that meant she was not going crazy. Her laughter slowly faded away and a frown creased her face. So, who was the old woman? And where was the baby? And why did Royce keep insisting neither existed?

Evening was approaching when Royce finally came back to the cabin. He was obviously exhausted, sweat gleaming on his chest and arms from his exertions. His face registered his surprise when he walked in the door.

"I...made dinner," Lindsey said, gesturing to where the table was set for their evening meal. She'd spent the afternoon cooking, relishing the activity that kept her mind busy. She'd analyzed and reviewed the scene with the old woman, the words that had been spoken, but she understood nothing and had finally pushed it to the back of her mind.

"I need a shower before I eat." He disappeared into the bathroom.

As he showered, Lindsey took the chicken and rice out of the oven. She'd been pleased to discover that his refrigerator and cabinets held a vast array of food.

She'd put the rattle beneath her pillow, unsure how to broach the subject of it, the woman in the woods and the baby. She had a feeling that if she asked him about them, he'd only lie.

She set the dish on the table, and with a spoon she tasted the rice, pleased that it was fluffy and tasty without being gummy. She took another bite, turning as she heard the bathroom door open. The rice stuck in her throat as Royce stepped out of the bathroom.

He was naked, a towel held at his waist, draping down in an attempt at modesty. His hair was slicked back, droplets of water still clinging to his shoulders and chest. In a fraction of a moment, Lindsey's eyes took in every inch of his physical presence. His skin looked eminently touchable, like a bronze statue. His legs were long, covered with dark hair, and she could see the lean lines of his hips, the taut muscles of his buttocks. The scar that ran down his flat abdomen only made him more masculine, like a warrior of ancient days.

She suddenly felt dizzy, all hot and cold and trembling. She wanted him. Despite all the rumors, despite all the things she didn't know about him, didn't understand, she wanted him.

"I forgot my other clothes." His voice was husky. His gaze held hers for a long moment, then he disappeared into his bedroom.

Lindsey expelled a tremulous sigh and sank down into a chair at the table. Strange how her fear of him was getting all mixed up with her desire for him. It was becoming more and more difficult to separate the two emotions.

She jumped as he came out of the bedroom, fully clothed, his face as usual an inscrutable mask. She got up from the table and poured the peas into a serving dish, then added the bread and butter to the table.

Once again she was aware of a thick tension building around them, a cocoon of suppressed emotion, a blanket of unspoken need.

"Would you like something to drink?" she asked, hesitant to join him at the table, afraid of the close proximity.

"No, I'm fine," he answered, but he didn't look fine. The muscle ticked in his jaw, causing the small mole on the side of his neck to move up and down.

"Maybe I should have made corn instead of peas. I really wasn't sure what you liked. I hope you don't mind that I took the liberty of making the meal. I know how hard you must have worked today." Lindsey knew she was rattling on, but she couldn't seem to stop. "I can put on some corn if you'd rather—"

"Lindsey." Her name exploded out of him, and she winced as he grabbed her wrist. His grip was painful, but it was the heat of his hand searing through to her bone that made her wince. "Everything is fine, just fine. Sit down and eat."

He released her wrist and she slid into her chair. The tension slowly eased as they ate. She wanted to ask him about the woman, show him the rattle and demand an explanation, but she knew instinctively he wouldn't tell her the truth. The swamp held secrets that for some reason he refused to tell.

"I couldn't help but notice the scar on your stomach. How'd you get it?" she asked curiously, wanting to glean what she could of this man of mystery.

He touched his stomach unconsciously, a small smile curving his lips upward. His smile held no bitterness, no anger, and Lindsey felt her heart lurch in her chest as his gesture eased the lines of his face and lightened the hue of his eyes.

"Most of the gators around here are fairly stand-offish creatures. They don't bother me and I don't bother them. But last year one particular big fellow took up residency in the water under this cabin." He paused a moment, his gaze drifting off to the side as he seemed to get lost in memory. "Every night he'd move right beneath the bedroom and bellow from dusk until dawn." He directed his gaze back to Lindsey. "Have you ever heard an alligator's bellow?"

She shook her head. "It's a horrible sound, rather like a bullhorn. The first night we thought it was funny. Monic—uh...I was told it was his mating call." He stumbled slightly, but had said enough for Lindsey to get a clear mental picture of Royce and his wife lying in bed, laughing about the mating habits of alligators.

"What happened?" The question spilled out of Lindsey, and Royce could tell that she was referring not to the cause of his scar, but rather to what had happened to Monica.

"After a week of listening to the gator, I didn't find it amusing anymore," he answered, his gaze letting her know he was intentionally misunderstanding her question. She let it go. This was the most he'd talked since she'd been here, and she had a feeling that in asking about Monica she would alienate him. He'd hide behind his shield of anger, and she'd learn nothing about the man behind the mystique.

"So, what did you do?" she asked, pushing her plate aside. She found his conversation much more sustaining than the meal.

"I decided I was going to move him, find him a home on the other side of the swamp where he could bellow to his heart's content."

Lindsey's eyes widened. "How do you move an alligator?"

"Very carefully." He flashed her a smile, exposing even white teeth. Lindsey felt her heart jump and skip a beat as she received the full benefit of the first real smile she'd ever seen from him. "I got rope and managed to wrestle him around until I got his mouth tied closed. Then I dragged him by his tail about a mile from here. I released him and managed to evade his snapping jaw, but as he struggled to get away, one of his feet managed to tear into my stomach."

"It must have been painful."

His eyes darkened, and he stared at her. For a moment his face was unguarded, vulnerable. "Sometimes soul wounds are much more painful than any physical ones can ever be."

The anger was back, surging inside him, painting his eyes in an uncanny light. He grabbed the bowl of peas, spilling some of the liquid over the side. "How about we talk less and eat more," he said with a growl. He effectively closed her out, concentrating on the food before him.

Lindsey watched him for a long moment, drawn to him more strongly than ever before. He could shut her out now, but he'd been too late. For just a moment,

while he'd stared at her, she'd seen his soul laid bare,
and it was a soul in jeopardy.

She had a feeling that in her was the power to heal
the inner wounds that afflicted him. What frightened
her was the uncertainty of reaching out to him. Was he
like the singing snake in his legend, drawing her in,
compelling her toward him only to strike out at her in
deadly fashion?

CHAPTER TEN

It was late. Royce had gone to bed hours before. Lindsey knew she should go to sleep, but she couldn't. Restless energy gnawed at her insides, moving her feet silently back and forth across the cabin's wood-planked floor.

With a sigh of frustration she opened the cabin door and stepped out onto the porch. The moon overhead played peekaboo, dancing impudently in and out of a thin, spotty layer of clouds. Its elusive light reflected on the pools of water in the distance, giving them a mirrorlike appearance. A light, cool breeze caressed her skin, ruffling her hair like a phantom lover's fingertips. Noise surrounded her, sounds that had become familiar. Like a mother's womb with a reassuring heartbeat, the swamp sounds enveloped her, comforted her.

When had it happened? When had she stopped fearing this place and come to love it? When had the strange noises become a rhythm that moved her heart, stirred her deep within?

She leaned against the porch railing, taking a deep breath of the pungent air. It smelled of mystery, greenery ... it smelled like Royce.

Royce...it was thoughts of him that made sleep elusive, evoked the restless energy that pulsated through her. At some time in the space of the past couple of days she had fallen in love with him. It was crazy, it was total insanity, but it was there. And this knowledge filled her with fear, despair...and finally a discomforting acceptance.

She closed her eyes, remembering his gentleness, the sadness in his eyes as he'd touched the dead fawn. She thought of the torment, the haunting despair he carried within his heart, and although her head told her differently, her heart believed it couldn't be possible that he had murdered a woman and a child.

"You'll destroy him." The woman's words came back to her, confusing in their content. What had she meant? Who was she and why was she warning Lindsey away from Royce? Was her intention to protect Lindsey or to protect Royce?

Lindsey remembered that brief moment at the table when his eyes had radiated a vulnerability that had pierced through her heart. Were his eyes those of a murderer? She didn't know, and that ate at her more than anything.

What she didn't know was if her love for him was enough to heal his inner wounds or if she would be pulled down into the darkness with him, losing herself forever. And what scared her more than anything was that she didn't care.

She had the feeling that whatever happened between her and Royce was going to happen no matter what. Their fate, whatever it might be, was preordained, and she was helpless to change the course of it. There was a power at work far greater than her will, a power that was compelling her toward him in dizzying fashion, leaving her no defenses.

He's bewitched me with his madness, she thought, lifting her face to the moonlight. He'd enchanted her, weaving a mysterious web around her, captivating her in his insanity. He'd pulled her down into his darkness where nothing mattered but loving him. This knowledge filled her with both wondrous joy and an overwhelming sense of despair.

She turned around and went back into the cabin, her feet automatically moving her toward his bedroom door. Perhaps if she saw him sleeping, saw that he was just a man and not some powerful entity who was slowly stealing her self-determination, perhaps then she could break the spell he'd wrapped around her.

She turned the doorknob and pushed open the door. It swung open without a creak. Despite the fact that she had not made a sound, he lay awake on the bed, his gaze on her as if he'd been expecting her. And as she stared at him, she knew she had not come to him in order to break the spell he'd cast on her; rather she had come in to descend deeper into the bewitchment he offered.

For a long moment they merely stared at each other, his eyes glowing like luminous green orbs, hypnotizing her, calling to her in a silent language all their own. And in his gaze she saw the future, the past, all elements of time and reality, fade away.

She knew she should run, knew she should flee both the passion and the violence he offered, but she couldn't. She was in a black hole, and the only beacon of light was Royce. At this moment, he was her reality and nothing else mattered.

As if in a dream, she moved to the side of his bed, then stopped, breathless as she waited for his reaction. His face was hidden in the shadows, the darkness a veil that hid his expression. She didn't know what to expect from him. She'd seen the fearsome power of his rages, and now she closed her eyes, suddenly very afraid of him.

''Lindsey.'' His voice was a silken thread, holding a sense of the same bewilderment that swept through her. She opened her eyes and looked at him once again, realizing he would not, could not turn her away any more than she could turn and walk away from him. He was as much a prisoner as she to the mysterious enchantment of the moment.

All doubts, all fears melted away and she knew with a certainty that this night between them was supposed to happen. The danger, the anger, the uncertainty of her very life merely heightened the tension that coiled like a hot wire in the pit of her stomach.

Without hesitation she unbuttoned the snaps of her jeans, the sound explosive in the silence of the room. They whispered down her legs and pooled on the floor where she gracefully stepped out of them. A strange quivering began in the pit of her stomach and again she wondered if she'd lost her mind.

She moved her trembling hands up to the top button of the chambray shirt, aware that in unbuttoning the shirt she was baring more than her skin. She would be exposing her heart, her soul.

As she unfastened the first button, Royce sat up. The moonlight streaking through the window slashed across his face, reflecting a hunger so profound it stole her breath away.

She moved to unbutton the second button, but his hand reached out and captured hers. For a moment his gaze held hers, and in the space of those seconds, she felt herself falling headfirst into the green depth of his eyes. Her soul left her body, and she closed her eyes, knowing he was now in full possession of her.

His hand pulled hers, drawing her closer, so close her legs were pressed tightly against the side of the bed. With one swift, strong motion he pulled her down on the mattress next to him. His naked chest was hot, burning through the material of the chambray shirt as he leaned over her. He took one finger and ran it down the side of her face, caressing first her cheekbone, then her jaw, and finally running sensually back and forth across the fullness of her lips.

The moonlight etched his features in bold lines and his eyes bore into hers, silently communicating his intense hunger, his desperate need. Lindsey felt a fevered heat sweep through her as her own need welled up inside, consuming her in a white-hot flame.

She captured his finger in her mouth, wanting to taste his flesh, devour him completely. Rational thought was no longer possible. She rode a wave of sensuality that made the thinking process virtually impossible.

He pulled his finger from her mouth, instead capturing her lips in a kiss of heady urgency. His lips pulled on hers, his tongue reaching within to stoke her inner fires higher. With a groan of impatience, he broke the kiss and threw the quilt that covered him off the bed.

In the moonlight, with his eyes glowing, he reminded her of an animal, wild, sleek and fully aroused. The sight of him, so strong, so masculine, so powerfully compelling, drew her farther into the darkness of his world. It was a darkness she didn't want to leave, a darkness she clung to, not caring if she ever crawled back up to the light again.

Her hands moved to unfasten the second button on her shirt. He pushed her hands aside impatiently. He grabbed the front of the shirt and with one swift motion, ripped it open, the buttons flying into the shadows of the room, rattling onto the floor.

Lindsey gasped at the barely contained violence of his action, her gasp immediately becoming a moan as his hands roughly covered her breasts. His thumbs moved maddeningly across her nipples, arousing her without touching her in any other way. As he caressed her for a moment, his touch turned tender, making her want more . . . more.

She felt a sudden bereavement as his hands left her, then his mouth was on her, hot and moist, tugging at her breasts, nipping lightly with his teeth.

She tangled her hands in his curtain of long, thick hair, feeling the heat and hardness of him as his body edged closer . . . closer. She pulled on his hair, wanting to draw him into her.

Lindsey trembled with a need that approached madness. Her body moved convulsively, trying to get under . . . over . . . inside his. She'd never known a need so intense, never felt the sort of mindless passion that was spinning her deeper and deeper into a velvet hole of blackness.

She cried out, a cry of surrender as his mouth left her breast, his hand trailing sensually down her rib cage, across her flat abdomen, then down to where she needed him most. His fingers teased her, lightly stroking her, the effect devastating her. She arched up to meet each caress, whimpering and pulling convulsively at his shoulders. She knew her fingernails were scratching his bare skin, but she didn't care, perversely glorying in the fact that she marked him.

She felt herself approaching an explosion and she fought against it, sensing a loss of self she could never reclaim. She was afraid, afraid of losing a piece of herself she could never get back in her possession.

But his touch held magic, and despite her attempts to maintain some modicum of control, she felt herself losing it, drifting closer and closer to the edge of a precipice. Without warning she was tumbling, falling over the edge, her body taut with swirling sensations as tears of pleasure choked in her throat, coursed down her cheeks.

He moved on top of her, intent on completing his initial possession, but Lindsey scooted aside, sitting up and touching his chest. She stared into his eyes, communicating to him that she wanted to give to him as he just had to her.

Apparently he understood her unspoken desire. The glow of his eyes intensified, and with a slight shudder he rolled onto his back, allowing her to take the dominant position. She met his mouth with hers, rubbing her breasts erotically across the hot, damp skin of his chest. She felt the tremor of his body and knew his tightly held control was slipping.

She pulled her mouth from his, kissing his neck, his breaths coming in uneven rasps. She loved the way he tasted, hot and wild. He smelled of green forests and elusive winds and she moved her lips down the hard muscles of his stomach, wanting to capture his taste, his scent forever in her senses.

Her lips moved on, finding and lingering over the scar tissue that slashed down his stomach. With the tip of her tongue she slowly traced the scar, feeling the convulsive tightening of his stomach, the growl he emitted deep in his throat. And when she moved even lower, his growl increased, and with a muttered expletive his control snapped. He pulled her back on the bed and covered her body with his.

His mouth took hers in fiery demand at the same time he parted her legs and entered her, heat meeting heat, iron against silk.

For a moment he didn't move, merely rested deep within her. He pulled his lips from hers and raised up slightly, his eyes glittering into hers. As their gazes remained locked, a bond was forged, a connection Lindsey knew would never really be broken. She was his, forever, for eternity. What was between them was more than physical, it was obsession, possession, a bonding of spirt and soul that she knew would mark her forever.

She tightened her legs around him, pulling him closer, deeper into her. She felt the tension radiating through him, felt him pulsating deep within her.

He moved his hips, slowly withdrawing, then filling her again and again. Lindsey again felt herself plunged into a void that held no time or space, no reality. His rhythm intensified and he tangled his hands in her hair, his thrusts almost violent and frenzied.

She reveled in his aggression, matching it with a fever of her own. She met his every thrust, her hands gripping at his shoulders, wanting to pull him into her, to melt into him.

Again she felt herself being pulled to the peak of a mountain, only this time she didn't go alone—she knew Royce was with her, climbing higher and higher. With a guttural groan, Royce stiffened against her, falling over the edge. Crying out, Lindsey followed him into an eclipse of darkness where their souls danced together, slowly melting into one.

Lindsey didn't know how long they lay together, their bodies still entwined. It could have been minutes. It might have been hours. She wasn't sure if she slept or not. The only thing she was sure of was her love for him, the feeling she had that no matter what happened now between them she would never be the same again.

And where did they go from here? She knew as little about him now as she had before. By making love to him she hadn't gleaned any more of the essence of the man than she had known. She knew now what his skin tasted like, how his flesh felt against her own. She now knew the power of his desire, but was no closer to understanding the source of his rage. And more importantly, she still didn't know what had happened to Monica.

She now lay across his chest, his heart thudding right beneath her cheek and ear. It was a slow, regular pulse, the heartbeat of a man momentarily at peace.

She closed her eyes for a moment, aware that she was about to break his peace. She hated to do it, but she wouldn't rest until she asked the questions she knew would stir the fires of his rage. She had to have some answers.

She stirred against him, raising her head to look at him. His eyes were closed, the lines of his face softer, but she knew he didn't sleep. She twined her fingers into his chest hair, dreading what she was about to do but knowing it had to be done. "Royce? Who is the baby?" she whispered, and felt him stiffen.

He drew in a deep breath, then expelled it slowly. It was not a sigh of anger as she had feared, but rather one of weary resignation.

"It's mine. The baby is my son."

Although Lindsey had suspected it, his words caused a gasp of surprise to escape her lips. He opened his eyes and again she saw they were filled with a torment so deep, so profound it frightened her. They were the eyes of a man who'd seen hell, perhaps been there, and the experience had marked his soul forever.

He raised up and she moved away from him, watching as he leaned over and lit the kerosene lantern on the table next to the bed.

Lindsey reached for the chambray shirt, which had been cast aside during their lovemaking. She pulled it on, buttoning the top button, then clutching the rest of it closed with her hand. She felt an inexplicable need to be covered, to hide from the lantern's glow illuminating the room. Or perhaps it was the death in his eyes that chilled her and made her need the warmth of the shirt.

She looked at him expectantly, loving him, wanting to erase the look of the damned that darkened his features, but also fearing him, unsure of his inner turmoil and how it might affect her.

With a swiftness of motion that startled her, he rose from the bed and reached for his jeans. He pulled them on as if he, too, felt the need for cover.

He drew his hands up to cover his face and when he pulled them down his features were twisted in savage bitterness. "Why are you doing this? Why are you picking at old wounds? Forcing me to remember things I've been trying to forget? Why? Why are you doing this?"

"Because I need to know," she whispered, apprehension once again racing through her as she saw the fevered glow of his eyes, felt the tension that suddenly vibrated in the air around him. "I need to know because I love you."

The words hung suspended in the air, and for a moment he didn't react. He turned his back to her, hiding his features from her, causing a dreadful anxiety to whip through her. She watched him, her body tensed, afraid of what he might do. Oh God, she shouldn't have said it, she thought, her breath catching in her throat as she waited for his reaction.

When he turned back to look at her, the fevered glow was back in the green depths of his eyes and his mouth curled upward in a gesture of pure, unadulterated madness. "And now your romantic heart can only hope that I love you, too." He threw back his head and laughed, the sound jarring and ugly, causing Lindsey to cringe, afraid that her words of love had somehow managed to push him over the edge, across the indefinable line between sanity and insanity.

He crossed the room, coming to stand before her, leaning down so his eyes glittered directly into hers. His breath fanned her face, and she recoiled, finding it not warm and provocative, but rather containing the coldness of a grave deep beneath the earth. "Are you sure you really want my love, Lindsey?" He touched her hair gently, almost lovingly, then reached out and grabbed her shoulders. "I loved Monica, and then I killed her."

"No." The denial escaped her in a hoarse whisper. "I...I don't believe you." It wasn't true. It couldn't be true. She couldn't love a man capable of murder. Her heart would know and refuse to allow her to love such a man, wouldn't it? "I...I don't believe you," she repeated with more conviction, but there was a horrible uncertainty that refused to dissipate.

His fingers dug deeper into her shoulders and he gave her a quick shake. "Believe it, Lindsey. I killed her. I murdered my wife." Lindsey cried out as his hands painfully gripped her. She struggled to get away from him, cowering in the face of his ugly anger.

He released his hold on her and grabbed her hand, yanking her out of the bed and to her feet. "And I'll tell you something else," he continued, half dragging, half carrying her toward the bedroom door. "I lied to you. The paths out of here have never been blocked. I could have taken you back to Cindy's place at any time."

Lindsey gasped, struggling to get away from him. She managed to break his grip as he pulled her into the main room of the cabin. She stumbled away from him, backing into a corner, staring at him in complete bewilderment. "Then why...why didn't you take me back? Why have you kept me here?"

Again a maniacal grin split his lips. "Because I wanted you. I wanted to taste the sweetness of your skin, feel your warmth surrounding me."

Each of his words ripped through her, tearing her apart. Had their lovemaking been nothing more to him than a physical want? An animal's need to couple? She didn't want to believe him, but his voice was harsh and cold, and his features were dark and forbidding, giving validity to his words.

He grabbed her jeans off the back of the chair and threw them at her, following them with her shoes. "Put those on," he demanded, his face demonic as he glared at her.

Trembling, suddenly afraid, she drew the jeans on and stepped into her shoes. She backed against the wall in an attempt to evade him as he once again grabbed hold of her wrist and dragged her toward the cabin door.

"Wait," she cried, tugging at his hand, fearful to go outside with him, terrified of what he intended. The momentary conviction she had that he couldn't have killed his wife was gone, and instead she felt cold, stark terror. "Where are we going? What... what are you doing?"

"I got what I wanted. Now I'm through with you." With these ominous words he pulled her out the door and down the porch stairs.

His grasp was an iron vise, pulling her into the darkness, into the tangled brush of the swamp. "Royce, wait." Panic welled up in her throat, tasting bitter and choking her. "Please... where are we going?"

His answering silence only fed her terror. Was he taking her back to Cindy's house, or was he taking her deeper into the swamp to a place from which she would never return? Was he taking her back home to safety or to her death?

She grappled against him in earnest, reason gone as she clawed at the hand that held hers so tightly, tried to kick at him in an attempt to get loose. He grunted as her foot connected with the back of his leg, but he didn't slow down, nor did he loosen his hold on her wrist.

He moved swiftly through the darkened swamp, the pale moonlight enough to guide him as he dragged her through thickets, around pools of water, over fallen limbs.

She fought like a woman obsessed, scratching his bare back, twisting her wrist in an attempt to break his hold, tripping as she tried time and time again to kick him. But, her efforts were futile.

In a final, desperate move, she reached up and grabbed a handful of his midnight hair. She yanked it with all her strength, letting loose a banshee scream to raise the dead. With a grunt of surprise, he momentarily loosened his grip on her hand. She pulled away from him, stumbling, crying out as she fell to the ground. She scrambled up, her heart threatening to explode in her chest as she ran blindly through the bushes, thorns and bristles reaching out to gouge and stab her.

She swallowed a cry as her foot splashed into cold water and images of alligators, jaws snapping hungrily, flashed through her mind. She veered in the opposite direction, her feet sliding in a patch of mud.

She heard him crashing through the brush behind her, calling out her name in thunderous tones. The sound of his anger-whipped voice spurred her on.

She ran like she'd never run before, her fear choking her throat, burning like hot coals in her chest. Tears streaked down her cheeks, more blinding than the shadows of night surrounding her. Still she ran, not caring where, as long as it was away from him, away from the danger Royce suddenly represented.

The swamp writhed and breathed around her, as menacing as the man who chased her. Audible above the sound of her labored breathing, a night wind whipped the trees, making them creak and groan like towering ghosts.

Rational thought was no longer possible. She was reduced to the most elemental emotion, the basic instinct of survival. Her veins sang the danger she felt, her heart pounding in excruciating pain as she searched for elusive safety.

She paused a moment, hiding behind the width of a large tree trunk, peering out, holding her breath in an effort to discern Royce's location. She heard him, close...too close, his breathing like that of a rampaging animal. Something slithered down the tree trunk near her head, and with a choked cry she turned and ran. She didn't look back, she didn't want to see how close he was to her.

She screamed, swiping at the cobweb shroud of Spanish moss that suddenly draped across her face, over her hair. It clung to her with tenacious fingers of film, like a spider's web capturing food. She swung her hands over her head, crying out once again as her feet slid out from under her and she hit the ground, the air whooshing out of her body. Panic squeezed her lungs as she gulped to regain her breath.

"You little fool." He appeared over her, a sinister tower of darkness and strength. With a thundering curse, he scooped her up into his arms and threw her over his shoulder.

Lindsey sobbed in despair, beating her fists impotently against the width of his back. She kicked her feet against the hard muscles of his stomach. But he seemed impervious to her efforts.

He walked forever, long after Lindsey had fallen into exhaustion, long after she had come to the dreadful realization that she was utterly powerless. If he was carrying her deeper into the swamp to kill her, then she would die. She was powerless to stop his madness, helpless against his rage.

His footsteps were long, measured, the walk of a man whose mind was made up, determined to accomplish whatever mission burned in his brain. And who knew what his fevered brain told him must be done? She sobbed in despair, berating herself for being such a fool, for believing in his sanity when it had been false.

It seemed a lifetime had passed when he finally stopped and eased her down off his shoulder. She looked around, shocked to discover they were on the edge of Cindy's manicured lawn. She looked up at him, bewildered.

His face was starkly highlighted by the moonlight, and for a moment she saw a vulnerability, a wistfulness that belied all his cold, harsh words. As quickly as she saw it, it was gone, swallowed up by an expression of threatening violence.

"Go," he exclaimed, giving her a shove in the direction of the house. Lindsey hesitated, the taste of fear still metallic in her throat, but the memory of that fleeting expression on his face holding her in place. His mouth twisted savagely and he shoved her once again. "Go back to your world, and stay out of mine."

When still she didn't move, he took a menacing step toward her, breaking Lindsey's inertia. A sob broke free, echoing in the utter stillness that surrounded them, then she turned and ran for the house.

CHAPTER ELEVEN

Lindsey expected dust to cover the furniture, cobwebs to hang in the corners, Cindy's cherished plants to be nothing but dead, dried leaves.

It seemed as if she'd been away for weeks…months. It was strange to walk through Cindy's back door and find everything exactly the way she'd left it. Nothing had changed, yet everything was different.

She walked around the house, touching odds and ends, running her hand over the back of the sofa, trying to grasp on to reality and separate it from the nightmare she'd just escaped.

She started to sink down onto the sofa, then spied the muddied footprints she'd tracked all over Cindy's carpet. "Damn," she muttered looking at the dark stains. She took off her filthy shoes and set them by the back door, then spent the next hour scrubbing all the muddied areas from the carpet.

The physical activity was welcome, keeping her mind off the myriad of emotions that had assaulted her over the course of the past several hours.

Carpet finally cleaned, Lindsey decided a shower was the next order of business. It wasn't until she stood beneath a warm cascade of water that she began to tremble. It began with her hands, then swiftly overtook her entire body until she was leaning weakly against the glass enclosure, quivering like a wind-tickled leaf on a tree.

Shock, some analytical portion of her brain concluded. She was suffering from the shock of terror sustained over three days. But shock didn't explain the tears that raced down her cheeks. Shock didn't begin to explain the aching bereavement she felt in her heart.

She scrubbed at her body until it felt raw, trying to erase the smell of the swamp, the feel of Royce that lingered in her pores. She wanted to forget him, forget everything that had happened to her since the storm.

She finished showering and wrapped herself in her bathrobe, lingering at the French doors of her bedroom to watch the sun rise over the mist-shrouded swamp. The sunshine chased away the early morning mist, leaving only fingerlike tendrils of fog as it spilled golden shafts of dawn onto the shadowed darkness. The brooding beauty of the sight caused a fullness in her throat, and once again she felt tears stinging her eyes.

She swiped at them impatiently with the back of her hands. She didn't even know why she was crying. She was home now, safe from harm, so why was she crying like a woman whose heart had just been ripped into pieces?

She moved away from the windows, unable to look at the swamp any longer. She went downstairs and curled up on the sofa, feeling more alone than she'd ever felt in her entire life.

Emotions swirled around in her head, all jumbled together. Her temples throbbed with a headache and she rubbed at her forehead in an attempt to ease the pain.

The lingering tinge of terror, the mystery of all the secrets, the ultimate possession of their lovemaking...all went around and around, battling each other for dominance in her thoughts, and she closed her eyes, as if in doing so she could silence them all. But it didn't help, and the emotion that kept coming to the surface was her fear of Royce and her love for him.

"God, what a fool you are, Lindsey Witherspoon," she gasped, tears once again welling up in her eyes. It was bad enough she'd once believed herself in love with a man of weak moral character. She'd been fooled by John, whose worst crime had been being a self-centered ass.

The love she'd believed she felt for John was nothing compared to the all-consuming strength of her love for Royce. How had it happened? How had she fallen in love with a self-professed murderer? Dear God, she should be arrested, put away for the rest of her life for her criminal lack of good judgment.

The man frightened her more than anyone had in her life, and she loved him more than anyone in her life. As she remembered the silent battle through the swamp as he'd brought her back home, she shivered uncontrollably, panic and terror still thick in her throat. She'd been lucky, so very lucky that he'd brought her back here and hadn't choked her to death and left her body to decay in the damp, thick brush of the woods. It would have been easy for her to disappear just like Monica had, leaving the town to speculate on whatever happened to that friend of Cindy Mae's who'd come to town to take pictures of the swamp. She shivered once again.

She took a deep, tremulous breath. It didn't matter anymore. Nothing mattered anymore. ''It's over now,'' she told herself, wrapping the warmth of the robe more closely around her. It was time to put it all behind her, forget all about the man in the swamp, his consuming rage, his deadly secrets, his mesmerizing passion. Like a nightmare with elements of fantasy, it had passed with the night and now it was time for her to face the light of day and reality.

''I thought maybe the storm had blown you away,'' Verla Sue exclaimed, offering Lindsey more coffee. The two women sat in Verla's kitchen, the scent of corn bread and seafood gumbo filling the air. ''I called and called but there was never any answer. I was so relieved when I finally got hold of you this afternoon.''

''I guess the phone wasn't working properly,'' Lindsey said evasively. ''Maybe something to do with the storm.''

Verla snorted. ''That's for sure. Somebody spits on these phone lines and they quit working. Anyway, I'm glad you could come to dinner tonight.''

''Me, too.'' Lindsey smiled, hoping Verla couldn't tell it was an empty gesture. It had been five days since she'd returned from the swamp, five days she'd spent in total isolation, trying to sort out her feelings and thoughts. She'd been pleased to accept Verla's invitation to dinner, needing to get back to a sense of normalcy, shove Royce completely and totally out of her mind and heart.

Verla jumped up and went to the stove, stirring the brew that simmered on the burner. "Wait until you taste my gumbo. You'll think you've died and gone to heaven," she exclaimed. "When my ex-husband and I divorced, he said the only reason he stayed with me the last year of our marriage was because he loved my seafood gumbo."

"It smells delicious," Lindsey agreed, stirring a spoonful of sugar into her coffee. She stared blankly at the dark liquid in her cup.

"Okay, what's wrong?" Verla sat back down at the table and looked at Lindsey critically.

"Nothing...nothing's wrong," Lindsey protested.

Verla narrowed her eyes, her gaze not wavering from Lindsey. "Look, I know I haven't known you very long, but it's long enough that I can tell something is eating at you. You're staring into your coffee cup as if you expect all the answers to the world's mysteries to be there. And those sighs of yours are so deep if I was to fall into one of them I'd never find my way out."

Lindsey smiled at Verla's description, then her smile slowly faded. "I guess I've just been thinking about what, exactly, I'm going to do with my life when Cindy and Remy return home." Although this wasn't completely the truth, it was a question that she had been considering for the past couple of days.

"I thought you were going to go back to Washington, D.C., and either try to get another secretary job or get those pictures of yours published."

Lindsey nodded. "Originally that was my plan." She fell silent, thinking of her options. "I always assumed that when Cindy and Remy returned I'd go back to my life in Washington, but suddenly I realize I have no life there." She thought of her apartment, full of things she didn't need. She thought of the people she knew, none of whom she could truly call a friend.

"Then stay here," Verla said, interrupting Lindsey's reverie. "You said you have some savings put away. Stay here and take your pictures, and if that doesn't pan out, get yourself a job here or in Cypress Corners." Verla reached across the table and patted Lindsey's hand. "I know Cindy would be thrilled if you decided to make your home here, and it would be nice to have a single girlfriend I could spend dateless nights with." She grinned dryly. "Although I doubt you'd have many dateless nights."

Lindsey smiled and sipped her coffee reflectively.

True to Verla's word the seafood gumbo was delicious. The conversation was light and pleasant, but even so, a sense of despair overwhelmed her as she drove home later that evening.

She'd hoped some time spent in Verla's company would help place her back in the here and now, break the silken threads of memory that kept part of her forever captured in the wilds of the swamp. But it hadn't worked.

As she drove, she once again found herself facing the question of her future. She didn't want to go back to D.C. There was absolutely nothing there for her. Nor did Verla's idea of remaining here in Baton Bay appeal to her. She wasn't sure she could survive living here, seeing the swamp every day, feeling Royce's presence, and not go stark-raving mad. No, neither of those choices seemed right, because her heart wasn't in them. She'd left her heart behind in a place dark and haunting with a man as mysterious as his surroundings.

She pulled the car into the driveway and got out, lingering in the last gasp of twilight. She watched as the black of night encroached, obliterating the last illumination of day. There was no longer any compulsion for her to hurry in, outrun the night. The night no longer held terror for her. It was only Royce, and her love for him, that terrified her.

And it was this that confused her more than anything, she thought as she went inside. If Royce was truly as evil as the people in Baton Bay believed, then why had he let her go? If he was really a crazed murderer, why hadn't he killed her? There would have been no witnesses, nobody to hear her screams. And if he really was all the horrid things everyone believed him to be, why did her heart not want to believe? On the other hand, if he *was* truly crazy, it was useless for her to try to make reason from his actions, glean sense out of the senseless.

She went upstairs and undressed, slipping on her nightgown, then opened the French doors and stepped out onto the patio.

A light breeze tousled her hair, causing her nightgown to dance sensually around her legs. The smells and sounds of the swamp wafted on the breeze, evoking in her a deep, piercing longing. A longing not so much for the place itself, but rather for the man...for Royce. Dear God, she'd truly lost her mind. Despite the fact that he scared her to death, she still wanted him.

She stared at the trees silhouetted against the night sky, wondering if he was someplace in the darkness, thinking of her. And was he thinking of her with love, or was he sorry he hadn't disposed of her?

Had he not harmed her because it wasn't in him to hurt anyone, and the stories and rumors surrounding him were just the gossip of small-town, superstitious people? Or had he merely managed to overcome his internal rage and murderous impulse to let her go free? There were so many questions, so few answers.

Surely he had felt the strange bond forged between them as they made love. She recalled how his hot skin had pulled forth a fever in hers, how his raging desire had fed her own. Perhaps he was the son of the devil, and what she needed was an exorcism to get him out of her head, banish him from her soul. She wrapped her arms around herself to ward off an inner chill.

With a heavy sigh she turned and left the patio, getting into bed. She left the French doors open, welcoming in the aura of the swamp. She no longer feared the thought of "swamp boogers" climbing in. She'd faced the king of the swamp and survived.

She pulled the sheet up around her and closed her eyes. She'd met the king of the swamp and gazed deep into his eyes. She'd recognized that he was damned. The problem was that in falling in love with him she had a feeling *she* was damned as well.

For five long days Royce fought his need for Lindsey. However, each night he found himself standing at the edge of the swamp, his gaze fixed on her as she stood on the balcony looking like a pale moonlit ghost in her long, white nightgown.

But she wasn't a ghost. She was warm flesh and fevered blood, bold courage and funny bravado. She was so vitally alive, and while she'd been with him she'd made him realize how dead he had been for the past year. He hated her for that. He hated her for reminding him of what he might have been.

He now stood hidden in the brush at the edge of Cindy's yard, watching the night breeze stir her hair, coveting the feel of her moon-kissed skin against his. He wanted to lose himself in the sweet scent of her hair. He wanted to again taste the passion of her lips, feel her legs wrapped tightly around him, pulling him into her heat and heart.

He'd loved Monica, but this thing with Lindsey transcended the mere mortal concept of love. She'd somehow managed to crawl inside him and touch him in a place he'd long held guarded and secret from everyone.

He'd known from the very first moment he'd seen her lying on the chaise longue by Cindy's pool that she was a danger to him. And when he'd gazed into her rich brown eyes, he'd known with a certainty that she was a threat to his tenuous hold on reality.

Even now, he felt his grasp on sanity slipping. He felt an overwhelming urge to go to her, take her violently, then do whatever was necessary to rid himself of her forever.

I should just let her go, he told himself as she left the balcony and disappeared into the house. Yet, even knowing this, his body trembled with his overwhelming need for her.

I will destroy her, he thought with dread. *Just like I did Monica. My love will destroy Lindsey.* But even as these thoughts pounded through his head, his feet propelled him forward, across the moon shadows of the yard.

Just one more time. He reached up and grabbed hold of the sturdy rose trellis that climbed up the side of the balcony. Just let me hold her one last time, then I'll do whatever it takes to get her out of my mind, he promised, pulling himself up and over the edge of the balcony.

His feet whispered against the wood of the patio as he moved to the open French doors. He stepped inside the room, standing for a moment to allow his eyes to adjust to the dimmer lighting. He saw her lying in bed, but as he stood there watching her, she sat up, her brown eyes widened with fear. Time stopped as they faced each other across the darkened room. Royce felt

the familiar rage filling him up inside as he saw her
moonlit beauty, felt his body responding with a vengeance. For a long moment he battled internally, unsure if he was here to harm her or make love to her. He
hated her for making him want her, he hated her for
looking at him with those liquid doelike eyes that
seared his soul.

He groaned as she raised her arms out to him,
beckoning him to her, speaking to him with her heart,
her soul. With a guttural groan, he crossed the room
and gathered her into the strength of his arms. For the
moment, his passion won over the rage, and he knew
at this instant that the only thing he wanted to do was
consume her, possess her.

His mouth claimed hers in a kiss that held a lifetime of hunger, and she responded by clinging to him
fiercely. Royce punished her with his lips, kissing her
brutally, harshly, his anger returning as she returned
his kiss.

"I shouldn't have come," he said angrily, tearing his
lips from hers, breathing in the scent of her.

"You shouldn't have stayed away," she countered,
her eyes no longer afraid of the hot liquid fire that
threatened to consume him. "Royce, I don't care what
happened in the past. I don't care what happens in the
future. All I know is that I love you. I love you."

He put his hand over her mouth, not wanting to
hear her pretty words that promised happiness,
knowing they were lies, all lies. There was no happiness, only pain and guilt, and again he hated her for
promising things he could never have. He moved his

hand off her mouth, again seeing the fear that darkened her eyes. He placed his hands on her throat, thinking how easy it would be to choke the life out of her, give full reign to the madness that licked his insides. He could feel her pulse beating in the side of her neck, erratic and wild with her fear.

She reached up and gently touched his face, and the madness momentarily fled, unable to withstand the onslaught of her tenderness, her love. He covered her lips with his once again, angrily taking what she offered, needing what she could give.

He paused only long enough to kick off his jeans and pull off her nightgown, then he plunged deep within her, his control gone as he possessed her completely.

Lindsey knew in some way he was using their lovemaking to punish her. From the moment he'd appeared in the doorway, she'd sensed his simmering anger, felt his trembling desire. Despite her fear, she'd held her arms out to welcome him because she had wanted him desperately despite her fear of him. She clung to him now, still feeling his rage as he tangled his hands in her hair, his lips ravaging hers.

As he moved rhythmically into her, his thrusts deep and powerful, Lindsey found herself transported to another place...a place of darkness and light, of mystery and knowledge, where she fragmented like an exploding star, dissolving into thousands of shooting shards. She clung to him, calling out his name over and over again, afraid that she would spin off the edge of the earth without him.

She was vaguely aware of him crying her name, joining her in the crazy spin as he burst within her. At that single instant she opened her eyes and looked at him, wonder and awe sweeping through her as she saw the tears that trickled down his cheeks. With her fingertip she caught one, putting her finger into her mouth, tasting the saltiness of the tear, wishing she could consume all his internal rage, all his pain, and heal the torment of his soul.

He collapsed on her, trembling in the aftermath. She trembled as well, too overwhelmed to speak. After a few minutes he moved his weight off her, withdrawing away from her and moving to the other side of the bed.

Lindsey turned to look at him, wanting to speak, wanting to tell him of the utter completeness she found in his arms. She wanted to tell him that she loved him as she'd never loved before. But his arm was thrown over his face and ominous tension radiated from him, and she was afraid to talk. When he pulled his arm down, his face held a savage anger that made her stomach tighten convulsively. His eyes glittered with the wildness that had haunted her dreams for the past five nights. He reached out and once again placed his hand around her throat, not exerting any pressure, but causing her breath to catch painfully in her chest.

"I've got to rid myself of you." His voice was flat, emotionless, frightening her more than anything she'd ever known. She knew he could feel her fear, and for the first time in her life Lindsey thought she might faint. But, just as she felt the blackness of terror de-

scending, he rolled up and off the bed. Without looking at her again, he pulled on his jeans and disappeared out the French doors.

A sob caught in Lindsey's throat, a sob of both relief and despair. For a long moment she didn't move,
afraid that he might come back in and follow through
on his promise. Her throat burned from the contact
with his hands. It felt so strange to have fear coursing
through her at the same time that the last lingering
sensations of desire had left her.

She must have slept, for when she awakened, the
light of dawn had crept into the room. She sat up in
the bed, wondering for a moment if the entire night
had only been a dream, a nightmare sort of fantasy
inspired by her intense longing for him.

She shivered, the early morning breeze caressing her
naked skin as it moved the gauzy curtains over the
French doors. No, it hadn't been a dream. The bed
beside her still retained the warmth of his body heat,
and in the slight depression where his head had rested
on the pillow, there was a pile of bright yellow ribbons. Her ribbons. All the ones he'd removed from
the trees the day she'd tried to use them as beacons to
find her way home. At some time while she'd slept,
he'd sneaked back into the room and left them.

Emotion clogged her throat and tears misted her
vision. She knew. She knew with a gut-wrenching certainty that it was his way of telling her goodbye. She
knew with a dreadful intuition that she would never
see him again.

And for the next three days she didn't. In those three days Lindsey felt her sanity slipping as she grappled with her love for Royce. Fantasy and reality meshed, becoming confused in her mind. She remembered his warnings, that once you entered into the depths of the swamp, you were never really the same again. She knew now that his warnings had been true, for she knew she'd been altered, transformed in a way that would never be undone.

The swamp was now in her soul. Its murky waters now ran through her veins. And it was the beat of the swamp's rhythm that pumped her heart, and her heart cried only one word . . . Royce . . . over and over again.

She found herself obsessed with the place and the man, needing to glean the secrets contained in the bogs. Who was the woman who'd dropped the rattle and warned Lindsey away? Royce had told her he'd killed Monica, but was it possible he'd lied? Was it possible that woman in the swamp was Monica? That something horrendous had happened that had made her go mad? Made her hair turn prematurely gray and her face age? She dismissed this whole idea, realizing it sounded like something from the pages of *Jane Eyre*.

No, in her heart she knew Monica was dead. But that knowledge answered none of the other questions that plagued her.

At night she stood on the balcony, calling to him with her heart, her soul. She tied the yellow ribbons to the balcony, letting them cascade like streamers, hoping they would beckon him back to her. She didn't stop to think that it was totally irrational to want a man she feared. She couldn't dissect her conflicting emotions—she only knew they existed.

And each night that she stood on the balcony, there was a moment when she knew he was near, watching her, wanting her. At those moments she felt his nearness, sensed his need, felt his aching torment and heard the way the night sounds all held their breath. But he never showed himself, never came to her. And she was both relieved by his absence, and heartbroken by it.

Finally, on the fourth night of her aloneness, she stood on the balcony, her thoughts whirling around in her head. Surely there was a logical explanation, a rational reason behind everything. She didn't want to believe that Royce had murdered Monica. She didn't want to believe him capable of such evil, but as she thought of the rage that was his constant companion, the angry way he had taken her body as if trying to destroy her, she just didn't know what to think. He was as contradictory as the swamp, offering stark beauty and hiding deadly components.

As she remembered the tears that had run freely down his face as he had made love to her, Lindsey knew she wouldn't rest, couldn't get on with her life until she knew the answers to the secrets of the swamp.

He was a man tortured, a man in torment, and she believed that somehow she was his healing, if only he would allow it. She also had to face the possibility that she was wrong, that he was too far over the edge into insanity to be saved.

She stared into the night, her eyes focused on the swamp, a feeling of resignation sweeping over her. She knew what she had to do. She had no other choice. Despite the fact that she'd been a horrible judge of character in her past, despite all the rumors and gossip she'd heard, she was going to return to the swamp. She had to learn the secrets contained there even if it meant she might never again return from its dark mysteriousness.

CHAPTER TWELVE

She headed out early the next morning, the sun warm on her shoulders as she made her way across the grass of Cindy's yard. She was well prepared for her journey. She'd found a sturdy duffel bag in one of the closets and had packed it with food items, a bottle of fresh water, a lightweight blanket, flashlight and matches.

She figured with these supplies she could survive three to four days alone in the swamp. Of course, she was desperately hoping that she would find the old woman before darkness fell. She'd come to the conclusion that the answers to the swamp's mysteries would be discovered by talking to the old woman. Lindsey just hoped she really could find her before dusk. She didn't relish the thought of spending the night alone in the swamp without benefit of shelter. But she would.... She would brave a million nights if the end result was discovering the secrets that haunted Royce, banishing the torment that held his soul captive. She had a feeling she would never find peace until she knew for certain if Royce was the man her heart wanted to believe he was, or if he was the evil entity the people of Baton Bay feared.

She had no idea what exact direction to take. It seemed reasonable to assume that the woman lived someplace near Royce, but she didn't even know how to get back to Royce's cabin. She'd been brought there while unconscious and when he'd led her away she'd been hysterical, too afraid to notice things like direction or reference points. Still she trudged on, depending on intuition, the Fates or some sort of divine intervention to guide her.

Initially it was pleasant going. The sun was warm, the air scented with hundreds of blooming flowers. She hummed beneath her breath, keeping her mind pleasantly blank, not wanting to think anymore about what she was doing, what consequences she might suffer.

She wished she had her camera. Her desire to capture the swamp's nuances on film had returned full-blown. But, as she feared when she'd been trapped in Royce's cabin, her camera had been ruined by the wind and the rain.

I'll get a new one, she promised herself. *I'll get another camera and sooner or later I will become a professional photographer.* She didn't stop to consider when or where she would take pictures again. At the moment, she had no future. There was nothing but her driving need of this moment.

By noon the going was less pleasant. Her shoes were mired in mud, and mosquitoes buzzed their annoying presence around her head. The scent of flowers was gone, overwhelmed by the more pungent odor of decaying plants and wet peat.

She found a relatively dry area and sat to eat a peanut butter and jelly sandwich, washing it down with gulps of water from the plastic bottle. When she finished eating she took a stick and attempted to clean off the mud that clung thickly to her shoes.

I must be crazy, she thought, aggressively attacking the mud with the stick. If Cindy Mae could see her now, she would have Lindsey proclaimed certifiable and put away for the rest of her natural life.

Lindsey readily admitted her lunacy. She'd been infected by Royce's insanity, and the frightening thing was she didn't care. She was on a sort of mission, a quest to regain her soul, and the only way to do that was to learn the truth about Royce.

Again she was struck with the thought that she was no longer in charge. Her free will had been stolen away by a pair of glittering green eyes and a love that filled her up, leaving no room for anything else except the fear that wouldn't go away.

She hadn't chosen her insanity. It had merely been a by-product of falling in love with Royce. However, she had a feeling that Royce chose to dwell in madness, and just as he'd made a conscious choice to be insane, she had a feeling he could also make a conscious choice to be sane. And if she was wrong? She shivered suddenly, finding that thought too dreadful to consider.

Shoes relatively clean, she pressed on, going deeper and deeper into the depths of the swamp. Birds squawked overhead, as if protesting her presence in their territory. The sunlight disappeared, finding it impossible to penetrate the thick trees and heavy brush that now surrounded her, and she knew she approached the very heart of the swamp.

It breathed around her, like a giant beast that had captured her in its jaws and swallowed her whole. She fought down a feeling of claustrophobic fear, knowing that if she gave in to it, she would go running blindly, screaming at the top of her voice. She paused a moment, took several swallows from her water bottle and a couple of deep cleansing breaths.

Feeling the momentary panic subsiding, she moved on. She made certain she made plenty of noise as she thrashed through the thickets, crashed through the brush, wanting all the slithery or furry creatures to hear her approach and hide. She had no desire to confront one of the swamp's inhabitants here in their natural environment.

She skirted the shore of a large pool of water, pausing a moment to admire the sight of several baby alligators swimming around a partially submerged log. She smiled. They looked so cute, so utterly harmless in miniature form. She stood watching the little reptiles as they cavorted. Terror widened her eyes as the benign "log" suddenly transformed into a huge alligator. It hissed, splashing and thrashing as it appeared to glide across the surface of the water toward where she stood.

Stunned, Lindsey watched its enormous jaws snap powerfully, a horrendous noise belching from their depths. It was easy to imagine those jaws clamping down on a leg, snatching off an arm. She heard screaming, and for a moment was disconcerted, unable to locate the source of the screams. Then she realized the source was her, and as the huge reptile emerged from the water, taking a step onto the shore where Lindsey stood, her inertia broke and she ran.

She ran until she was no longer able to scream, her breaths coming in quick, painful gasps. When she thought she'd gone far enough, she stopped running and leaned over, trying to catch her breath. With trembling legs, she sat down and pulled out her water bottle. She drank deeply, then splashed a little of the tepid water onto her forehead.

God, she'd been a fool to brave the swamp on her own. She had no idea where she was, no idea which direction to travel. She didn't even know how to get back to Cindy's.

She took a deep breath, realizing there was a hush surrounding her, an unnatural hush that made her hold her breath in anticipation. She looked around. "Royce?" she called tentatively, wondering if he was near, watching her. Was he laughing at her? Knowing she was helplessly lost and would probably never find her way out of this place? Or was he waiting for her to stumble onto a secret place of his, a place where he could finish the threat he'd made to rid her from his life?

A tree frog croaked nearby, and it seemed to be a signal, for immediately the natural swamp sounds returned. Had he been near, or had the silence merely been a natural one? God, she didn't know anymore what she believed.

She looked at her wristwatch and realized it would be dark in the next couple of hours. Although she dreaded the very thought, she knew she needed to find a place to spend the dark hours of the night.

It took her almost another hour to finally find a place she thought suitable to stay. In the middle of a small grove of evergreen trees, the ground was relatively dry and the sturdy trees would provide a little cover from any night wind that decided to blow.

She gathered dried twigs and branches, thinking a fire was a necessity and would probably keep any curious night creatures away. Feeling as prepared as possible for night to fall, she sat on her blanket, eating crackers and cheese and an apple, wondering when exactly it had happened that she'd lost her mind.

Perhaps it really had been the blow to her head. She reached up and touched the still-tender area on her forehead. Maybe the accident had caused more than just a mild concussion. She thought of the crying baby, the woman she'd seen twice in the wooded area around Royce's cabin. Had they been real? Or had they only been a figment of her imagination?

She shook her head and pulled the blanket up around her shoulders. They had been real. Royce had told her the baby was his, and his words had validated the fact that a child truly existed. Lindsey had held in her hand the rattle that the old woman had accidently dropped. It too, had been proof of the child's existence. And it seemed reasonable to conclude that the woman and child must live near Royce's cabin. But where?

As she tried to light a fire, she thought of Royce, a perverse anger seeping through her. Every other time she had entered the swamp, he'd always appeared as if by magic. But this time, when she most wanted him to come to her, most needed him to help her find her way, he was nowhere to be found. How like a man, she thought irritably.

Night didn't come slowly to the swamp like it did to other areas. There was no warning, no gradual deepening of the shadows. One minute it was day, the next it was night. Lindsey was grateful for the fire as the darkness closed in around her. She moved closer, not so much for the warmth but toward the light, needing it to chase away her fear.

She stared into the fire, wondering where Royce was, what he was doing. Was he thinking of her? Wanting her? Or had her feelings of a soul connection between them only been a fantasy... the wistful imaginings of a lonely woman? Had other women felt a bonding just before they were killed by men crazed with anger? She thought of the tears that had coursed down his face as they had made love. Tears that had spoke of an inner pain so tremendous she couldn't comprehend it. But were those tears evidence of a man who wasn't crazy? Or were they the tears of a man who was completely crazy? She rubbed her hands over her face, tired of thinking, tired of trying to make sense out of the whole mess.

She jumped as a strange noise split the night, coming from someplace close on her left. It was a primal sound, a noise that had no place in civilization, no place in this century. She shivered and moved even closer to the fire as the noise continued. It was a rhythmic sort of bellowing that shattered the silence of the night and caused goose bumps to appear on her arms. There was something about it that sounded mournful...sad.

She relaxed as she suddenly realized what it was. Of course, it was the mating call of an alligator. As she listened to it, she felt a sort of empathy with the reptile. She, too, wanted to bellow her pain and loneliness, hoping to draw Royce to her just as the alligator hoped to attract a female gator.

She froze, her adrenaline pumping as she discerned another sound hiding just beneath the thunderous notes of the gator's song...the wail of a baby. She turned her head, trying to discover the direction of the cry. Yes...there it was, coming from her right, riding on the breeze that blew it from that direction.

Her heart thudded anxiously as she kicked wet peat over her fire, dousing the flames. She grabbed her flashlight from the pack and turned it on, the beam barely illuminating the ground in front of her feet. She stood for a moment, listening intently, hearing beneath the rapid beating of her heart the crying child.

Surely I'm close, she thought, picking her way through brush, shoving through thickets and brambles. With each step she took, the sound seemed to get closer and her heart pounded louder in her ears.

Bats darted overhead and the bellowing alligator's cry grew more distant as she continued. She only hoped that she wasn't following a distorted sound, that it really was coming from the direction where she was headed and wasn't some perverse trick of the swamp.

She cried out in relief as she stumbled into a clearing where a small cabin sat, light streaming out of the windows. She stood at the edge of the woods, staring at the cabin in both fascination and dread. She was certain this was where the sound of the baby had emanated from. She was equally sure that this place probably belonged to the old woman. But now that Lindsey was so close to having her questions answered, she wondered if she really wanted the answers.

What if the old woman only confirmed what the people in Baton Bay said? What if she told Lindsey that Royce was a crazed madman who murdered his wife in cold blood?

Perhaps the best thing to do was to turn around and go back to Cindy's. Leave the questions about Royce unanswered, one of the universal mysteries that remained a mystery.

Even as this option crossed her mind, she dismissed it. She couldn't let it go. Royce had become an obsession she couldn't turn away from. She had to find out the truth. She had come too far, loved too deep to turn and walk away from it all now.

Taking a deep breath, she slowly made her way to the door of the cabin. The moon cast dark shadows onto the cabin, giving it an ominous aura. A witch's house, she thought suddenly. The place looked like what, as a child, she'd imagined a witch's house would look like. It was the kind of place where Hansel and Gretel had nearly been eaten by the wicked witch.

Her feet made no sound as she moved across the peat, hesitating at the bottom of the three wooden stairs that led up to the door.

She grabbed the stair railing, but before she could take another step, the door flew open. The old woman stood in the doorway. Her face was hidden in shadows as the light behind her silhouetted her form. "I've been expecting you," she said, opening the door wider. "Well, come in if you're coming," she exclaimed impatiently, then turned and left the doorway.

Lindsey hesitated a moment, then slowly moved up the stairs and entered the cabin.

CHAPTER THIRTEEN

As Lindsey passed over the threshold and into the cabin, she felt as if she'd passed through an invisible doorway that separated the real world from a place of dreams.

Like Royce's cabin, the old woman's home consisted of one large room with two doorways leading into smaller rooms. Unlike Royce's cabin, this one boasted a huge, stone fireplace that took up the space of one entire wall. Despite the relative warmth of the night, a fire was lit, filling the room with heat and light and a faint smokiness that only added to the otherworldly aura.

There were plants everywhere. They hung from the rafters overhead, grew profusely in an oblong flower box at the window. They filled the room with vivid color and fragrance. There were herbs, too, strange-looking roots and berries that emitted a strange pungent odor.

"Have a seat, the tea is almost ready." The old woman gestured to the table. Lindsey slid into one of the wooden chairs, her gaze still darting around the room. The furniture was simple wood, with a primitive beauty, and a nearby bookshelf held half a dozen books...journals of some sort, from the looks of them.

She felt as if she'd somehow slipped through a crack, fallen into an alien warp that had thrown her back in space and time. There was something so primitive, so elemental about the old woman and her surroundings.

With her long black dress and flowing gray-tinged hair, the old woman looked like a pioneer...or a witch. Lindsey shifted uneasily in the chair at this last thought.

She watched with interest as the woman removed a battered iron teakettle from the grate in the fireplace. With a deftness born of habit, the woman poured two cups of water into stone mugs, then carried them to the table, placing one in front of Lindsey.

Lindsey looked into the cup suspiciously, frowning as she saw the strange seeds and leaves floating around in the water. The old woman watched her, then cackled in glee. ''Don't worry, it's just harmless herbs. No evil sleeping potions or poisonous plants.'' As if to prove the point, the woman took a sip from her own cup, smacking her lips in apparent satisfaction, then looked at Lindsey expectantly.

Lindsey took a tentative sip, surprised to find the brew slightly bitter, but not unpleasant. She got the impression that she was somehow participating in a ritual of some kind, a ceremony she didn't understand. She took another drink of the tea, feeling the old woman's dark eyes perusing her, studying her for some indefinable purpose.

She knew instinctively that the old woman was in control, that no questions would be answered until she was good and ready and felt Lindsey was worthy of knowing the answers.

So Lindsey waited, patiently drinking her tea while her mind whirled with the questions she so desperately wanted answered.

There was no sign of a child, and the sound of crying had disappeared the minute Lindsey had walked through the doorway and entered the cabin. She felt a moment's panic as she wondered if it had all been some sort of strange hallucination. Had it been a trick? A ploy to get her here?

Perhaps it wasn't Royce who was the crazy one of the swamp. Perhaps Monica had sat in this very same chair, drinking this very same blend of tea, and had been killed by the woman sitting across from Lindsey, her dark eyes reminding Lindsey of other eyes... dark eyes that had radiated threat and danger. Maybe Royce was merely protecting this crazy old woman...maybe...

Lindsey mentally shook herself, again feeling as if she'd entered into some strange dreamworld where nothing was as it seemed and reality had no place.

The silence lasted between them until both their mugs were empty. "I knew you would come." The old woman finally spoke, her voice sure and steady. "I knew it because Obediah told me."

"Obediah? You mean the fortune-teller in Baton Bay?" Lindsey asked curiously.

The woman's wrinkled face creased with the lines of a sly smile. "Obediah has about as much fortune-telling powers as dogs have wings." Her smile slowly faded. "'Course, every once in a while she gets things dead-on right, and she was definitely right about you. The minute she heard that you planned on coming into the swamp, she knew you'd be trouble. And Lordy, but you've been trouble." She looked at some imaginary spot above Lindsey's head. "It's like history repeating itself all over again... all the pain and the blood."

Pain and blood... At that moment, as Lindsey stared at the old woman, she recognized where she'd seen those eyes before. The old woman sitting before her shared common physical traits with the fortune-teller who had scared the hell out of Lindsey. "Who are you?" she asked, her voice a mere whisper.

The woman focused her gaze back on Lindsey, a small smile playing on her lips. "I'm Opal. Obediah's sister... Royce's mother."

Shock rippled through Lindsey, and she stared at Opal incredulously. Royce's mother.... Lindsey would have never made the connection on her own. For some reason, she'd just assumed that Royce's mother was dead. She'd heard the rumors about Royce's mother being a witch, but the implication in Baton Bay had been that the woman was dead, that Royce now lived here in the swamp all alone. Lindsey stared at her, unsure what to say, how to react.

"We tried to keep you out of here, Obediah and me. We tried everything we knew how to make you go away." Opal heaved a deep sigh, one that embodied a misery so deep it made Lindsey's insides quiver. "Obediah tried to keep you away when she told you your fortune. She wanted to scare you enough so you'd keep out of the swamp. Then we put that voodoo doll on your stoop, hoping you'd go back to where you came from. But you're a stubborn one, aren't you?"

"But why?" Lindsey asked. "Why try to keep me away? I wasn't doing anything to harm anyone. All I wanted to do was take some pictures."

"Ah, but that was before you and Royce met." Opal got up from the table, her hands worrying themselves with the folds of her dress. "You're just like her, just like the last one who came here. She nearly destroyed my boy. And you're just like her. You'll be the death of Royce."

"No, you don't understand. I'll be his life," Lindsey countered softly.

Opal snorted derisively, her eyes dark and haunted. "That's what I thought about the other one. I thought Monica would be his salvation, but she was his damnation."

"Tell me what happened. Please...I need to know."

Opal looked at Lindsey for a long moment, her eyes ancient, as if she'd seen enough pain and heartache to last ten lifetimes. "Ah, you love him." There was a note of sad resignation in her voice. "I was afraid of that." She looked at Lindsey speculatively. "You've heard the stories about him in town?" Lindsey slowly nodded her head. "And you still fancy yourself in love with him?'' When Lindsey again nodded, Opal snorted one more time. ''Yes, the other one, she was the same way. She heard all sorts of crazy stories about Royce and didn't have enough sense to be scared.''

''The stories I heard were nothing more than the superstitious nonsense of ignorant people,'' Lindsey exclaimed, then couldn't help adding, ''weren't they?''

Opal shrugged. ''Those stories are powerful, hurtful ones when you're a child laboring beneath them.'' She heaved a deep sigh and moved over to a wooden rocking chair that sat before the fire. She eased herself down and closed her eyes, the only sound in the room the soft, rhythmic creak of the chair as it moved back and forth. Lindsey found herself wondering if the chair was one that Royce had built. The workmanship was magnificent.

For a moment she thought Opal had fallen asleep. She was just about to call out to her when Opal opened her eyes and heaved another deep sigh. ''I suppose in order for you to understand what happened between Royce and Monica, you need to know a little about Royce's childhood. He hasn't always had that core of bitterness, the burning anger inside him.'' Opal looked at Lindsey knowingly. ''You've seen it, haven't you? The evil anger that twists his soul, that makes all God's creatures still and cower when he passes by?''

Lindsey nodded, a cold chill suddenly dancing up her spine, forcing her to wrap her arms around herself in an effort to still it. Yes, she'd seen Royce's rage, felt the power of the anger that ate at his heart, threatened his soul. She'd seen it and she feared it. She pulled her chair up closer to the fire, needing the warmth to permeate her body.

"He didn't always used to be that way." Opal set her rocking chair back in action, a smile curving her lips as her eyes hazed in memory. "Royce was a good boy, bright and happy, active and always asking questions about everything. He always loved the swamp, was never afraid of anything out there." She hesitated, folding her hands in her lap. "When I sent him off to Baton Bay to school, I knew the town had silly prejudices against those of us left here in the swamp. I figured Royce could win them over, rise above the malicious gossip." Her smile slowly disappeared and she shook her head sadly. "But I'd forgotten about the cruelty of children. Sure, they were just mouthing the things their parents were saying at home, but that didn't make the words sting any less. Many was the night Royce would cry because of the things the others said about his mother and father, about him. And how I cursed those stupid people with their stupid gossip."

Opal got up and poured herself another cup of tea, offering more to Lindsey who shook her head. The older woman returned to her chair, took a sip of her drink, then continued to speak. "By the time Royce was in high school, he'd become all the things they told him he was. He withdrew deep inside himself, quit school and pulled the cover of the swamp more securely around him. He trusted nobody, didn't think he needed anyone other than this place. The only person

he's maintained a friendship with is Remy Clairbourne—they went to school together.''

"Remy?" Lindsey digested this bit of information
with interest.

Opal smiled once again. "Remy is a good man. I
think there must be some swamp people in his family
tree. He comes here sometimes and shares a cup of tea
with me. Of course, I don't have much use for that
wife of his, but Remy has been a good friend. Royce
often works for Remy's construction company. He'll
work anyplace except Baton Bay. He has no use for
that town or its people.''

So, Royce didn't just spend his time alone in the
swamp making furniture. He worked for Remy. That
might explain how he had gotten into the house the
night he broke her camera lens. If he and Remy were
that close, then probably Royce had a key to the
house. "But what happened to Monica?" Lindsey
asked impatiently. Although she found each new tid-
bit of information about Royce fascinating, she was
anxious to get to the heart of the mystery. She needed
to know if Royce had really killed his wife.

Opal sipped her tea, her gaze thoughtful as it lingered on Lindsey. "You remind me of her. Oh, you
don't look much like her, but you have the same energy, the same curiosity, the same vitality that drew
Royce to her. By the time Monica came into the
swamp, Royce had pulled into himself so deeply I
thought nothing and nobody would ever bring him
out. But she did, and for the first time in years I saw
Royce happy." Her dark eyes misted over. "Monica

gave Royce hope, made him believe he wouldn't spend
the rest of his life alone, scorned and feared as the
Swamp Man.'' She was interrupted by the cries of a
child coming from one of the other rooms. Opal
wearily pulled herself up and out of her chair. ''Poor
little mite is teething. He hasn't managed to sleep
through a night for the last week.'' She disappeared
into the next room.

Lindsey waited only a moment, then followed her,
drawn to the sound of the child . . . drawn to Royce's
son. She entered the darkened room, her heart aching
with a strange, powerful need.

The bedroom was small, with a single bed against
one wall. Against the opposite wall was a crib, and
standing in the crib, his little chubby hands grasping
the rails for balance, was a beautiful dark-haired child.
Big tears rolled down his cherubic cheeks, and Lindsey noticed his eyes were the deep green of a forest.

''Maybe he cries because of the teething pain, or
maybe he cries because his mama is dead and his
daddy is so filled with anger he won't let himself get
close to the child,'' Opal observed as she watched
Lindsey move closer to the crib.

''May I?'' Lindsey didn't wait for an answer. She
moved across the room and held out her arms to the
child. The little boy looked at her for a long moment,
then he laughed, a joyous burst of childish delight,
and reached for her.

Lindsey cuddled him close, breathing deeply of the
scent of innocence that clung to his baby skin and hair.
And as he reached up and tangled a hand in her hair,

Lindsey realized that this miniature version of Royce had already managed to crawl into a special place in her heart. She kissed the top of his forehead, smiling as one of his hands latched onto her nose.

She followed Opal out of the bedroom, sitting down in the rocking chair as Opal indicated she should. As Opal busied herself fixing a bottle, Lindsey cuddled the little boy in her arms, stroking his face as he watched her with curious eyes. "What's his name?" she asked.

"He's a baby without a name. His mama couldn't name him and his daddy wouldn't. I call him Reese, after my own daddy."

"Reese." Lindsey smiled as the boy responded by grinning and reaching once again for her hair. "It's hard to believe one little boy can generate so many crazy stories," Lindsey observed, taking the warmed bottle from Opal and watching as Reese drank greedily. "They told me in town that Royce had murdered his son, that phantom cries of the dead baby can be heard when the wind blows."

Opal nodded. "That's a story Obediah started telling everyone to protect the child. 'Course, a story like that, it didn't take long for it to spread like wildfire."

"Protect him from what?" Lindsey asked curiously.

Opal sighed impatiently. "Think, girl. What do you suppose all those well-meaning hypocritical matrons of Baton Bay would do if they discovered there was a child out here being raised by the Swamp Man and his crazy witch of a mother?" She walked over and angrily stirred the fire with a poker. "They'd take him away, that's what they'd do. Take him and stick him in some foster home where he'd learn to hate and fear the very man who fathered him."

Lindsey looked down into the green eyes so much like Royce's, and her arms tightened protectively around him. He squirmed against her constraints, wanting her to hold him, but not too tightly.

Lindsey smiled, seeing Royce's strength and independence already in the little boy. Her smile slowly faded. "You still haven't told me exactly what happened between Royce and Monica . . . about how she died."

Opal added another log to the fire, poking at it once again. She eased herself back down in a chair, looking old and weary. She closed her eyes and tipped her head back. "There's a storm coming," she said, as if she hadn't heard Lindsey. "I can smell it on the wind." She opened her eyes, one hand moving to rub her kneecap. "I can feel it in my bones."

Lindsey realized she was right, the wind had picked up, howling around the sides of the small cabin. Lindsey felt a different kind of storm building within her, one of impatience. Would she ever get the answers she sought? Before she could say anything, Opal spoke again. "Royce and Monica were so happy until she realized she was pregnant. That's when everything started to change."

"Royce wasn't pleased about the baby?" Lindsey guessed, looking down at the little boy who'd fallen asleep in her arms, a dollop of milk clinging to his chin.

"Lord no, Royce was thrilled. He wanted children, lots of them, to fill up that cabin. It was Monica who wasn't happy." Opal sighed and once again rubbed her knee. "As the pregnancy went on, she got real melancholy and weepy. She cried at the drop of a hat, sat for hours staring out at the swamp. She started having nightmares and would wake up screaming that the baby was going to kill her, that she'd never escape this swamp, and her body would rot here."

Opal paused, tragedy etching her face in deep lines. Lindsey took the opportunity to shift the child in her arms.

"He's sleeping sound. I could take him back to bed now," Opal offered.

Lindsey shook her head, unwilling to relinquish the child. She leaned down and kissed his forehead. "He's fine. Please go on."

"Well, Royce and I, we tried to comfort Monica as best we could. We told her that her crazy feelings, her nightmares, all of it was probably just hormone stuff, her body reacting to the pregnancy. Royce took her into a doctor in Cypress Corners and he assured her everything was fine. But the bigger she got, the worse she got in the head. Finally, when she was about eight months gone, she demanded Royce move out of the swamp and take her with him. She was crazy, ranting and raving and out of control. Royce had been patient for eight long months, but this time he lost his patience. They had a terrible fight and he left, spent the day brooding alone in the swamp." The lines in her face seemed to visually deepen. Again her hands sought the folds of her skirt, as if finding comfort in grasping the dark material.

"We don't know what happened next," she continued. "Royce left, I came back here. Later on that evening I walked back to their cabin to check on Monica." She leaned her head back and closed her eyes. "I smelled it first before I ever got through the door. The smell of blood, lots of blood. It's something you never quite get out of your nose. I found her lying in a pool of blood, the baby just born, but pitiful weak." Her hand trembled visibly as she rubbed it across her forehead as if trying to erase all the bad memories there. "I tried to save them both, but Monica had lost too much blood. Royce came in, he held her, he begged her to hang on, but she died in his arms."

"Then Royce didn't kill her," Lindsey exclaimed, joy surging inside her. Tears of relief welled up in her eyes. Her heart had been right all along. He hadn't killed her—it had all been a tragic accident of fate. A tragic accident that had deprived a man of his wife, a child of his mother.

"He might as well have killed her for all the grief and anger he carries inside." Opal got up, taking the poker and stirring the fire once again. "He blames himself for not taking her fears more seriously. He blames himself for not moving her to Cypress Corners where she'd be closer to the hospital. And he's angry that fate taunted him, showing him a glimpse of what happiness can be, then snatching it away.''

"But he could find that happiness again with me," Lindsey said softly, meeting Opal's gaze and holding it.

"Perhaps." Opal looked at her speculatively. "You're strong, I'll give you that. And you have to be, to love a man like Royce. But are you strong enough to leave your life behind and live here in the swamp? Are you strong enough to have people gossip about you?"

"Yes." Lindsey answered simply, knowing no other answer was possible. She would rather live here in the swamp with Royce than anywhere else on earth without him. Without Royce, she would be nothing more than one of the walking dead, a zombie without a heart, without a soul.

She stood up, cradling Reese in her arms. "This child needs his father, and I need Royce. Will you take me to him?"

"Now?"

Lindsey nodded urgently. It suddenly seemed vital that she not wait another minute—another second— to go to Royce. Her heart told her that he needed her as desperately as she needed him.

Opal hesitated a moment, then disappeared into the bedroom, returning with a satchel. "Here are the boy's things." She looked longingly at Reese. "I love him, but you're right. He needs his daddy. I'm old and I'm tired, too tired to be raising him." She took a shawl from a hook by the door and laid it across

Lindsey's shoulders and Reese's sleeping form. "Let's go then," she said brusquely.

Opal was right about an approaching storm. As they stepped outside the cabin door, lightning sizzled in the distance and the smell of imminent rain danced on the cool wind. Lindsey turned on her flashlight against the utter blackness of the night.

"We'll have to hurry," Opal said, looking up into the dark sky. She limped down the three stairs, obviously favoring her right leg. "The storm has put a misery in my bones," she muttered as they started up a path.

Within minutes of walking, it was obvious that Opal was in genuine pain. She limped, moving more slowly with each step they took. She finally turned to Lindsey, her face drawn and white. "I can't go on," she said, leaning down to rub her knee. "My leg won't carry me much farther. It's easy to find from here. Just stay on this path and as you come to the forks, go left, then right, then left again. You'll see his cabin from there."

Lindsey wanted to throw herself at Opal's feet, wrap her arms around her legs and beg her to take her the rest of the way. But she knew the old woman was hurting. Besides, she had a feeling that it was meant to be this way. For some reason it felt right that she should come to Royce with his child, having made it through the swamp alone.

A gust of wind whipped her hair, ruffling the shawl and making Reese whimper in his sleep. She secured the shawl more firmly around him, then on impulse she reached out and hugged Opal. The woman stood stiff and unyielding, but finally gave in to the embrace, awkwardly patting Lindsey on the back.

"Left, then right, then left again." Lindsey repeated the directions as she released the old woman.

Opal nodded. "If you change your mind, just reverse yourself."

"Why would I change my mind?"

Opal shrugged. She started to leave, then hesitated and turned back to face Lindsey. Her features were somber, her dark eyes flickering with a trace of something Lindsey thought might be fear. "The man Royce once was, he was a good man. He would have never hurt anyone." A jagged streak of lightning rent the darkness, and with the sudden illumination Lindsey knew it was fear radiating from Opal's eyes.

"Opal?" Lindsey felt an answering tremor race up her spine.

"I fear for you. I fear the man my son has become. I pray his heart hasn't turned black and cold beneath the weight of his anger and guilt. I fear for your mortal life... and I fear for his soul." With these ominous words, she turned and disappeared into the darkness of the night.

CHAPTER FOURTEEN

For a long moment, Lindsey stared at the spot where Opal had been, allowing the old woman's words to penetrate her head.

Had Royce's anger and pain suffocated all the goodness in his heart? By going to him now would she finally irrevocably push him over the edge? Would he allow his anger to consume him and take her life? Would it be a self-fulfilling prophesy and he would become what everyone believed he already was?

"I fear for your mortal life." The words of his mother caused her to shiver with apprehension. But despite her anxiety, despite the fear that tickled her insides, she had to see this through to its conclusion.

Lightning split the clouds overhead, and they crashed back together with a resounding boom. Reese jerked convulsively in her arms, wailing his fear, and Lindsey knew she must hurry to outrun the storm.

She ran, the child clutching at her with frantic hands, his cries exploding out of him in terror. The wind picked up in intensity, breathing a frenzied life into the dark surroundings. The light the flashlight cast was weak, unable to penetrate the darkness that closed around them like a shroud. The cypress trees moved and groaned, as if trying to prevent her passing. Branches reached out, clutching at her with their thorny fingers. The swamp writhed around her like a hungry, frenzied beast.

She stumbled, crying out as she caught her balance, but lost her grip on the flashlight. It clattered to the ground in front of her, its light immediately dousing. "Damn," she shouted, reaching down for it, hoping it had shut itself off in the fall. But when she clicked the on/off button, nothing happened. She tucked it into the satchel, knowing she would have to rely on the flashes of lightning to help guide her.

She hurried on, feeling the first warning splatters of cold rain on her face. She cuddled Reese more firmly against her body, his cries eerie as they rode on the crest of the fierce wind.

Finding the first fork in the path, she took off to the left, once again running, her chest heaving with her exertions.

She ran for what seemed like a lifetime, slowing down only when she thought her heart would explode out of her chest. She paused a moment, panting to catch her breath, wishing Reese would stop his crying.

She'd lost all track of time. Had she missed the second fork? Was she going in the wrong direction? Dear God, was she lost?

Panic squeezed her insides. "Royce!" she cried, needing him, afraid she would never find him, afraid she would die out here with his son in her arms. But the wind took her cry and mockingly threw it back in her face. "Royce," she tried again, not knowing if it was rain or tears that suddenly streaked down her face.

It's like my dream, she thought suddenly, remembering the vision that had so haunted her, the nightmare she'd suffered on the night she'd found her camera lens broken. In that dream she'd been running in the swamp, fighting the elements, racing for her life. But what had confused her was that when she'd awakened from that nightmare, she'd had the distinct feeling that she'd been running into the swamp, toward Royce and all his madness.

I'm living my dream, she marveled, and in that knowledge came a certain kind of peace, a certainty that she was doing what fate compelled her to do. She'd seen her future in her dream, and she knew she was following the course destiny had mapped out for her. At the same time these thoughts came into her head, she saw the second fork.

A strange, dreamlike fog enveloped her as she calmly made her way down the narrow, overgrown path. The lightning flashed, thunder roared, but Lindsey whispered soothingly to the child in her arms, knowing the swamp wouldn't harm them. She was part of it, and she *knew* she would be all right. She felt it beating in her heart, knew that she was a part of it as never before.

Within minutes, she broke into the clearing and stared at Royce's cabin, a mixture of anticipation and dread coursing through her.

Her dream had shown her that she was supposed to be here, but it hadn't shown her what the results would be. She had no idea what to expect. The certainty of her coming here disappeared, replaced by a dreadful uncertainty.

Reese had stopped crying, as if he knew they'd reached their final destination. Taking a deep breath, without giving herself a chance to think, to change her mind, she went up the porch stairs and pushed open the cabin door.

He'd apparently been sitting at the table carving, but as the door creaked open he shoved back his chair and stood up, facing her with the wrath of an angry warrior flashing on his face. "What are you doing here?" he asked, his voice a crash of thunder to compete with nature's noise. Lightning flashed in his eyes as he saw the child she carried in her arms. Lindsey's arms instinctively tightened protectively around the child.

For a moment, the urge to run back outside overwhelmed her as she saw the violent intensity radiating from his mysterious green eyes. But, as she remembered the tears that had escaped those eyes as he'd made love to her, the tenderness he'd shown a dead doe, the urge to run passed. She would never run from him again. "We've come because this is where we belong," she said.

With a calmness that hid her erratic heartbeat, she walked inside and closed the door behind her. Feeling Royce's gaze on her, she lay Reese down on the cot, covered him with the shawl and gave him his bottle. The child immediately closed his eyes, exhausted by the trauma of the past few minutes in the storm. She moved two of the chairs from the table over to the cot, their backs providing a barrier so the child wouldn't roll off the bed. She leaned down and stroked his peach-soft cheek, then straightened up and looked at Royce.

She sucked in her breath as she saw the savagery on his face, felt the dangerous tension that rippled in the air around him. "This child needs his father, and you need him."

"He doesn't need me," Royce scoffed, his face a twisted mask of bitterness. "A child needs a father who is whole."

Lindsey's heart ached at his words, so full of despair and hopelessness. "Royce..." she advanced toward him, trying to still her trembling as she saw the rage that filled his eyes, consumed his features.

"You were a fool to come here." His words hissed out of him on a breath filled with wrath, and again Lindsey felt a tremor suffuse her body.

She faced him resignedly, knowing her eyes reflected the love in her heart. "Your son isn't the only one who needs you.... I need you."

Her words seemed to unleash his turbulent emotions, and with a strangled cry of torment he grabbed at her, wrapping his hands tightly around her neck. His eyes flashed the fires of hell as his hands constricted painfully. She didn't fight him. She'd already given him her soul, so what did it matter if he choked the life from her. As he squeezed the air from her throat, the only emotion she felt was an irrational self-anger. She'd been wrong again. She'd thought it impossible that he would hurt her, but she'd been wrong.

"I could kill you," he rasped, his eyes orbs of hell's damnation.

"And I would still love you," she managed to gasp out.

For a long moment he didn't move, didn't appear to breathe, then he suddenly jerked his hands away, releasing his grip on her neck. He crumpled, falling on his knees to the floor. He covered his face with his hands. "Help me." His whisper was a cry of anguish and desperation. "Dear God, please help me."

His words ripped through Lindsey's heart, and she sank to her knees in front of him, gently removing his hands from his face. Tears welled in her eyes as she saw the utter despair that marred his handsome features. She touched his face, placing her fingertips on either side of his cheeks, staring deeply into his tormented eyes. "Let me help you. Let me love you."

"I'll destroy you." The words escaped him like a sigh.

"Like you destroyed Monica?" When he tried to jerk away from her, she laid her palms on his face, refusing to let him go. "Royce, Monica's death was a terrible tragedy, but it's one you aren't responsible for."

"I should have listened to her fears, I should have moved her into Cypress Corners." His voice was raw with emotion, his eyes deep wells of suffering.

"And there is no guarantee that the end result wouldn't have been the same. You could have had her at the hospital and she still might have died. Royce, you can't go back and rewrite the past. It's over, it's done. It's time to let go, let go of your anger and guilt and live again.''

"I don't know how." Anguish deepened his voice.

"Let me help you," Lindsey replied, and she leaned forward and kissed him, her lips containing all the love, all the healing power she possessed.

With a muttered groan, he pulled her into him, his kiss filled with such longing, such tenderness that tears again misted Lindsey's eyes. "I should send you away from here, away from me, but I can't," he moaned, raining kisses on her mouth, her eyelids, her forehead. "I can't send you away because I do need you, Lindsey. God help me, I love you." He stood up and swept her into his arms, his gaze not wavering from her as he carried her into the bedroom.

He laid her gently on the bed and took off his clothing rapidly, as if afraid if he didn't hurry she would disappear like a puff of smoke. While he undressed, Lindsey did the same, also feeling that urgency, needing him more desperately than ever before.

When he rejoined her on the bed, their warm flesh melted together, their hands and lips hot as they sought each other's secrets. There was no time for thought, no need for words as their bodies moved together in a dance of timelessness.

Where before a violent intensity had colored their lovemaking, this time there was nothing but tenderness, nothing but their love between them.

As the storm raged its power outside, Lindsey used the power of her love to show him what their future together could be. She loved him with her mouth, her entire body, and she also loved him with her heart, her soul. He met her tenderness with tenderness, caress for caress. When he finally entered her, gasping her name over and over again, Lindsey cried, knowing that this was the first time they'd made love not only with their bodies, but with their hearts. And afterward, as they lay in each other's arms, listening to the gentle rain whispering its rhythm on the roof, Lindsey knew she was where she belonged.

She awoke some time later, her body still tightly entwined with his. Dawn crept into the room, bringing with it a shimmering streak of sunlight, a promise that the storm from the night before had passed.

She raised her head, for a moment watching Royce's face while he slept. Her love blossomed up inside her like a flower opening to the sun. She knew there would still be rough times. Royce had closed himself off for too long for her to believe that in a single night he would be truly healed. But she also knew that he'd opened himself up enough to allow her in, and with time and love he'd believe in happiness once again.

She silently moved from the bed, not wanting to disturb him, needing to check on Reese. She grabbed a shirt from Royce's closet and threw it on, then quietly crept from the room. Reese was still asleep, a chubby leg sticking out from the cover of the shawl. She tucked his leg back in, pausing a moment to touch the silkiness of his baby-fine hair. This man and his child, yes, she would love them both. Together they would be a family, a family whose strength could withstand the silly gossip of a town full of superstitious people.

She stepped outside onto the porch, breathing in the scent of the rain-sweetened morning air.

This place had called to her the moment she had seen it, a mystical call she'd been unable to ignore. She didn't know anymore if it had been the song of the swamp or the soul of the man who lived here that had compelled her. It didn't matter, for she loved both.

She leaned against the railing, listening to the sounds of the tree frogs, the distant splash of a fish breaking the surface of a pool of water, the lazy buzz of insects, the scurrying of an animal in the nearby brush. Yes, she loved this place and felt the contentment that could only come with being home. Home.

She turned at the sound of the cabin door opening, smiling as Royce stepped out and joined her on the porch, wrapping his arms around her and pulling her close against him. "I thought you might have been a dream," he murmured into her ear. "I thought I'd dreamed it all and I would wake up and find myself alone. And then I saw Reese, and I knew it wasn't a dream and you were really here."

"We're real, and we're here to stay," she assured him. "You're never going to be alone again."

For a long moment they stood in each other's arms, their hearts talking softly to each other without a word needing to be said.

He sighed deeply. "I didn't want to love you. God
knows, I tried not to. I wanted you to go away. I tried
to make you go away." He reached his hand up and
lightly caressed her hair. "I couldn't scare you, but
you scared the hell out of me. I was so afraid you'd
come, and so afraid you wouldn't. I'm so afraid you'll
stay, and that you'll leave." He paused a moment, as
if finding the words to express his emotions difficult.
"It frightens me, loving again." He looked into the
distance, then back at her. "Lindsey, I can't ask you
to sacrifice your life to live here in the swamp with me.
I... We could live someplace else...maybe Cypress
Corners..." His words were tentative, and if Lindsey
had any doubts about his love for her, they banished
them.

She looked deep into his eyes, loving him for the
sacrifice he'd been willing to make for her. But she
knew the swamp was as much a part of Royce as the
heart beating in his chest, and to ask him to live anywhere else would be to tear out a piece of his soul.

"We'll live right here, Royce. You and me and
Reese. I love this place, and Reese will learn all its
beauty and dangers. We'll be a family."

"Are you sure?" He seemed to hold his breath.

"I've never been more sure of anything in my life."

He expelled a contented sigh. "Imagine...the
Swamp Man with a family. You know, the people in
Baton Bay will think you've been bewitched by me."

She smiled up at him. "I'll tell them it's true. You
have bewitched me, and I intend to stay in that state
for the rest of my life." She reached up and kissed

him. "And I'd like to remind you, you still owe me a new camera lens."

He laughed, a pleasant rumble. "You've got a deal," he agreed.

Lindsey smiled, knowing the cancerous rage inside him was gone. For as they stood there, arm in arm, the swamp sounds didn't silence, they swelled like a symphony as if each and every creature embraced the two lovers in approval.

* * * * *

And now,
an exciting preview of

THE LAST CAVALIER
by Heather Graham Pozzessere

Look for THE LAST CAVALIER and two other
haunting Silhouette Shadows™ romances
available this month.

And every month from now on, watch for
the new Silhouette Shadows novels,
stories from the dark side of love,
wherever Silhouette books are sold.

CHAPTER ONE

Blackfield's Mountain
September, 1862
Before...

The Confederate cavalry officer stood staring down Blackfield's Mountain, his gloved hands on his hips, his silver-gray eyes fixed on the field stretching out below him. His plumed hat sat low over his brow, concealing any emotion in his eyes from his waiting men. He knew how to command, how to be stern, how to be merciful. He knew how to instill his men with courage, while also doing his damnedest to keep them all alive.

A spasm of unease suddenly crept along his spine. There was something he didn't like about the day. It was early morning; but already the battlefield was nearly black with powder from Yankee mortar and Confederate Napoleons. A man could barely see two feet in front of his face.

There seemed to be a promise of rain from the heavens above. The distant clouds, which had grown as black as the powder of cannon fire, seemed to billow and roil in a constant, wild commotion. Yet here, where he stood, the day seemed unbelievably still.

A tempest was coming. A tempest deeper than battle, louder than any clash of steel. It seemed as if God himself had grown angry with the fratricide and was about to grumble out his wrath. There was something ethereal about the air. Something tense, something charged with a strange lightning . . .

Something ghostly. . . .

But Jason Tarkenton had been given the order to charge, and so he would.

Today, both the Yanks and the Rebs would be forced to use their cavalry units to fight. The enemy had been gathering in the valley, preparing to attack. He would have to take the initiative.

"Charge!" Jason ordered.

"Yessir!" rose the voices of his men.

Jason's saber slashed through the air as he stretched low over his horse's neck, leading the advance.

He felt the hoofbeats pound beneath him, the vibration of the earth as over a hundred mounts followed hard behind him. Ahead of him lay the enemy in blue. Men and boys. Some would fall, and some would die. And soon, somewhere, someplace in time, mothers would cry and widows would grieve. And that was what war was: death and despair. But a man was called upon to fight it, and it was best not to dwell on the pain and horror.

Jason swore when a cannon shot exploded right in front of him and he was thrown from his horse. The air was so thick with the explosion of powder and earth that he couldn't see a damned thing. A wind had risen with the cannon shot. A strange wind. One that seemed to come from both the east and the west.

No, the wind couldn't come from the east and *the west, especially not when the day had been dead calm just a few minutes ago. Dead calm, with a leaden gray sky.*

But despite the strange wind, the powder swirl that had filled the air did not settle. It seemed to grow. Odd. There was a loud crack in the sky, like the sound of a cannon, but distinctly *not* the sound of a cannon.

He stared skyward. Clouds billowing black and gray, seemed to rush down toward him. There was an arbor of large oaks just to his side. Huge trees that reached the clouds themselves, their branches forming an archway. The clouds curled back into themselves, puffing and swirling in the archway formed by the swaying branches of the trees. He realized in amazement that a strange doorway had been created in the arbor, in the blowing clouds and mist.

All around him strange winds rose, and in their whistling gust he heard a mournful wail, a cry that seemed to echo from the very heart of the dark twisting heavens. The lashing branches moved like gigantic bony arms, mocking him, beckoning him closer, into their skeletal embrace. And as he watched, an unearthly sensation swept over his body from head to toe, as if someone—or something—was touching him. Touching him with clammy fingers that trailed a chilling path down the length of his spine.

The sounds of battle grew dim, as if the fighting was taking place in the far-off distance—as if he heard no more than a memory of those sounds.

Jason couldn't see a thing. He pushed himself up from the ground and stuck his arms out into the black mist, trying to feel something ahead. He didn't have time to wait for whatever this was to blow over. He had to keep walking.

The trees! There they were ahead of him. The trees where the clouds had created a shadowy passage through the darkness and the mist. He had to reach the trees.

The wind picked up violently. He didn't need to walk toward the trees; he was being swept there.

Fingers! he thought wildly for a moment. Yes, it was as if the bony fingers of some huge, unnatural hand were reaching for him, dragging him forward. He gritted his teeth, trying with all his strength to push against the funneling winds. But those fingers had captured him in their damp, bone-chilling grip. It was like living a nightmare, feeling himself suspended in time, trapped in the twisting darkness of this unearthly tempest. The winds howled around him like the mournful voices of lost souls, their chill screams like babbling curses hanging in the air.

He was a soldier in Lee's great army of Northern Virginia! he reminded himself, shaking off the feelings. He had to be afraid of Yankee guns and sabers, and he had to rage against any strange winds that stood in his way.

Keep moving! But even as he moved, the earth seemed to shift beneath his feet. Then all of a sudden it was as if he'd walked into a brick wall. He veered back, tripped and started to roll.

"Damnation!" he muttered. Bony fingers be damned, tempests be damned, with his luck he'd roll right into a Yank troop.

The blackness swallowed him. He was a part of it now, he thought. He reached out desperately to stop himself.

His head hit a rock, and stars burst inside his mind. The trees! He had come between them; he was rolling beneath the branches that touched the skies. Now they, too, with long, bleached white, bony fingers, seemed to reach and stroke and scratch at the sky.

Later he opened his eyes. For a moment, he lay still. He was still on the mountaintop; he hadn't gone very far.

And yet things were different. The blackness was gone. As if he had blinked it away. He looked up. The sky was a vivid blue, and the sun was blazing golden. He could hear a whistle, but no eerie moans, no sounds of battle.

"What the bloody hell is going on?" he muttered aloud. Had he been unconscious so long? He had thought he'd barely blacked out—just seconds.

He started to rise, but then he heard someone calling out, and he ducked down. Staring downhill through the long grasses, he could see row after row of tents. Army-issue, Union tents. Cooking fires blazed away between the tents, and delicious aromas rose from pots hanging over them. Men and women mingled.

The women were in simple cotton dresses; few seemed to be wearing petticoats. They were well dressed for army-camp life. The men were in blue. Yankee-issue blue.

Jason pressed his palm against his temple. Damn, it seemed he had stumbled into the main portion of the Union army!

Quickly, Jason crawled behind a large boulder and leaned back against it. He closed his eyes. How had he come here? And just where the hell *was* here?

Blackfield's Mountain
Now...

Vickie smiled sweetly at the six old men filling her grandfather's tiny tavern and reminded them, "The war ended quite some time ago, you know. Well over a hundred years ago now! It was 1865, remember?"

The men grinned sheepishly.

This was a big week for the small Virginia mining town. Not only would the battle the men were arguing about be reenacted on Saturday, but already some of the largest reenactment encampments ever drawn together were being set up in Miller's cornfield right alongside the mountain. Everyone in town was involved in the reenactment in some way.

Of course, Gramps had always been a major-league Civil War buff. And therefore, she thought, so was she. He had gleefully decided that with all the tourists in town, they should dress just like the reenactors. There sat Gramps, wearing a Virginia militia field uniform, and she was walking around serving coffee and beer in a long antebellum dress. Gramps wanted to get the folks into the spirit of the festivities when they came in for their sandwiches and drinks.

Glancing up at the clock, she saw the afternoon was gone. "Do you need me anymore, Gramps?"

"No, honey—you run on out and see your friends." He hesitated and added gruffly, "You still going to the Yankee camp?"

Vickie had to laugh, setting a kiss on his bald head. "Gramps, the war is over! And I hate to tell you this, but they did win, you know!" She heard him grunt, and she rose, winking at his comrades.

"If I were you, young lady, I'd take that little filly of yours rather than driving. They aren't letting any cars into the fields where the tents are pitched. Since they have a bunch of the historical-society types coming, they're trying to make everything look authentic."

She wasn't all that far from the encampments, and Arabesque could certainly use the exercise. She kissed her grandfather again. "'Night, Gramps."

"Don't you fraternize with them Yankees too long."

Vickie smiled, then passed from the taproom into the entryway of the house. In the dim light, she caught sight of her reflection in the wavery hallway mirror. She definitely looked the part that Gramps had asked her to play. Her simple cotton gown had a high-buttoned bodice and a small frill of lace along the wrists, neckline and hem. It was pretty, and the dark plaid went with her deep auburn hair and blue eyes.

Leaving the house, she walked around to the rear of the old barn and into the stables. Arabesque was a beautiful Arabian mare. In the deep and painful confusion that had haunted her after her husband's death, Vickie had roamed the endless blue and green fields and forests of the Virginia countryside on the sweet, spirited creature, and she'd come to know a certain peace. Now she mounted her beloved mare and rode off.

She hadn't gone very far before she realized that she'd truly left the light of civilization far behind. She was well accustomed to this country, but this night seemed exceptionally dark. There was no moon above to light her way. She reined Arabesque to a stop, suddenly seized by an eerie feeling of impending danger.

"How can I be afraid?" she mocked herself out loud. But it was dark. Awfully dark.

And no matter what she told herself, a feeling of unease had taken root inside her. Arabesque seemed uneasy, as well. She suddenly whinnied, then reared. A night breeze picked up, strong and wild.

There was a blur in the darkness, and suddenly a figure leapt out from behind a rock. A man.

Vickie shrieked in terror as Arabesque reared wildly again, pitching her over backward and then running off. She heard a mumbled intonation of fury from the man, and she tried to get up, but rough hands held her by the shoulders, then dragged her to her feet.

She knew she should be afraid. But the fear hadn't sunk in yet. She was staring at him, realizing that he was very handsome. She noticed his cavalry hat then, and the large sweeping plume that protruded from it. His uniform was gray wool with yellow trim. Southern cavalry. Authentic, right down to the dust and gunpowder marks.

His hands clamped over her mouth. She started to struggle but suddenly found herself held tightly in his arms. She felt the simmering fire of his eyes as they stared warningly down into hers.

"Sorry, ma'am. But you aren't going to get me caught!"

Caught? Wasn't he taking this playacting just a little too seriously? She twisted, kicking him in the shin. She was furious, but now panic was beginning to seize hold of her, too.

"All I wanted was your horse, but I've lost that now. I really don't mean you any harm, but I'll be damned before I'll let any Yankee-loving woman get me tossed into a prison camp for the duration of this war!"

Suddenly he bent low and butted her belly with his shoulder, throwing her over his back. The air was knocked clean from her. She gasped, desperate for breath. She couldn't scream, couldn't breathe. And he was running, with her weight bearing him down, heading for the trees that rimmed the crest of the mountain....

SILHOUETTE® *Shadows*™

Welcome To The
Dark Side Of Love . . .

COMING NEXT MONTH

Take 4 bestselling love stories FREE

Plus get a FREE surprise gift!

SHADOWS FREE GIFT OFFER

To receive your free gift, send us three proofs-of-purchase from any Silhouette Shadows™ books from March, April or May with the Free Gift Certificate properly completed, plus a check or money order (do not send cash) for $2.25 to cover postage and handling, payable to Silhouette Shadows Promotion Offer. We will send you the specified gift.

FREE GIFT CERTIFICATE   096 KAN

Name: _____

Address: _____

City: _____ State/Prov: _____ Zip/Postal Code: _____

Mail this certificate, three proofs-of-purchase and check or money order for postage and handling to: Silhouette Shadows Promotion, P.O. Box 9071, Buffalo, NY 14269-9071 or P.O. Box 604, Fort Erie, Ontario L2A 5X3. Requests must be received by June 30, 1993. No liability is assumed for lost, late or misdirected certificates.

PLUS—Every time you submit a completed certificate with the correct number of proofs-of-purchase, you are automatically entered in our HAUNTING SWEEPSTAKES to win the GRAND PRIZE OF A THREE-DAY TOUR OF SALEM, MASSACHUSETTS, for two, including accommodation, airfare, sightseeing tours and $500 spending money. No purchase or obligation necessary to enter. See below for alternate means of entry and how to obtain complete sweepstakes rules.

HAUNTING SWEEPSTAKES
NO PURCHASE OR OBLIGATION NECESSARY TO ENTER

To enter and take advantage of the SHADOWS Free Gift Offer, complete and mail your Free Gift Certificate, along with the required proofs-of-purchase and postage and handling charge, to: Silhouette Shadows Promotion, P.O. Box 9071, Buffalo, NY 14269-9071 or P.O. Box 604, Fort Erie, Ontario L2A 5X3. ALTERNATIVELY, you may enter the sweepstakes without taking advantage of the SHADOWS gift offer, by hand-printing on a 3" × 5" card (mechanical reproductions are not acceptable) your name and address and mailing it to: Haunting Sweepstakes, P.O. Box 9069, Buffalo, NY 14269-9069 or P.O. Box 626, Fort Erie, Ontario L2A 5X3. Limit: one entry per envelope. Entries must be sent via First Class mail and be received no later than June 30, 1993. No liability is assumed for lost, late or misdirected mail.

Sweepstakes is open to residents of the U.S. (except Puerto Rico) and Canada, 21 years of age or older. For complete rules, send a self-addressed, stamped envelope (WA residents need not affix return postage) to: Haunting Sweepstakes Rules, P.O. Box 4682, Blair, NE 68009

To collect your free necklace you must include the necessary proofs-of-purchase with a properly completed offer certificate.

ONE PROOF-OF-PURCHASE

096 KAN

Limited